Who Stole
Kathy Young?

A **CAT'S EYE** Mystery

WhoStole Kathy Young?

by
MARGARET
GOFF
CLARK

SCHOLASTIC BOOK SERVICES
New York Toronto London Auckland Sydney Tokyo

For Fanny Church Goff, my mother

ACKNOWLEDGMENTS: The author wishes to
thank: Jeff Messinger, County Extension Marine
Agent, Aransas County, Texas, for information
on shrimp fishing and for checking the manu-
script; Sister Virginia Young, Principal, and her
staff of St. Mary's School for the Deaf, Buffalo,
N.Y.; Shelley Rowe, Hearing Aid Specialist,
Huntsville, Ontario, Canada.

ISBN 0-590-32165-X

12 11 10 9 8 7 6 5 4 3 2 1   10   2 3 4 5 6/8

CONTENTS

The Staring Stranger

Rusty growled low in his throat.

Startled, Meg Carberry looked across the rough stretch of sand and saw again the dreaded figure of the man perched on the low wall that separated the Youngs' lawn from the beach.

He was wearing shorts that displayed his bony legs and, as always, a cap with a long, pointed visor. When he stood up, so tall and thin, Meg's heart gave a panicky leap. He was looking directly at her.

Then, deliberately, the man climbed back over the wall and strolled away across the grass.

The big Chesapeake Bay retriever, one year

old and full of spirit, tugged on his leash. A ridge of rust-colored hair bristled on his spine.

Meg held him back. "This way," she urged, pulling him toward the road. Although she had a reputation for being fearless, not for anything would she go closer to that man.

It was a perfect early June morning. Already the Texas sun was hot on the sand, and the bay was bright blue with white-fringed waves. It was the first day of summer vacation and the beginning of a two-week visit with her best friend, Kathy Young.

Kathy had been asleep in the other twin bed when Meg, awakened by Rusty's barking, slipped out to exercise her friend's dog.

When she hurried up the curving drive toward the house, the dog was still making short muttering growls and glancing back toward the tall man who was now sauntering north on Shore Road.

It was only when Kathy, with her long black hair flying, ran down the drive toward them that the dog changed his growls to excited yips of pleasure. Meg let go of his leash and he bounded forward. He was friendly to almost everyone, and he always obeyed Mr. Young, but Kathy was the center of his world.

Meg went on past them toward the house.

On the front terrace, Mrs. Prentice was setting the table for breakfast. Her indignant voice greeted Meg as she came up the steps. "So you're the one who made that dog bark this morning. Don't you realize some people need their sleep?"

Meg was surprised, even though she was aware of the housekeeper's crusty disposition.

Before she had a chance to explain that Rusty had awakened her, too, Kathy called out behind her, "Hi, Meg! Where'd you go? You were gone when I woke up."

Meg whirled around and said with a smile, "Your dog took me for a walk."

Mrs. Prentice vanished into the house, taking an unwilling Rusty with her. Of course Kathy wasn't aware of the woman's remark because she couldn't hear well enough to catch a conversation if the speaker's back were toward her. She wore a hearing aid, but still she needed to pick up some words by reading lips. It was no use making Kathy unhappy by telling her what had been said.

The housekeeper brought out the electric coffee pot and plugged it in. "An extra person to feed and then we have to eat out here," she complained, keeping her voice just low enough so Kathy couldn't understand her.

Meg flushed, and her gray eyes showed the hurt she was determined to hide. She stood up even straighter than usual and kept her gaze on Pedro, the Mexican gardener, who was under the largest live oak tree, raking up the few fallen leaves, shiny and oval like dehydrated minnows.

Just then Kathy's father came out of the house. "Morning, everyone!" He strolled over and put his arm around Meg's thin shoulders. "And a special good morning to my second daughter. Seems real fine to have you around."

Meg leaned her head against him for a brief moment, all the anger draining away. This tall, dark-haired Texan with his understanding brown eyes was one of her favorite people. She knew Daniel E. Young was an important man in the nearby village of Oak Point and in all of eastern Texas, but to her he was simply a friend, a grownup friend with whom she felt completely comfortable.

Now that her employer was there, the housekeeper's personality changed like a chameleon.

"Just the day for eating outside," she said with a put-on smile.

Mr. Young pulled out a chair for the woman and she sat down and unfolded her napkin. Meg wondered if Kathy's father would treat her like one of the family if he could see the real Mrs. Prentice that lurked behind her smile. She had come here only a month ago

4

when Mrs. Anderson, the former housekeeper, had gone to live with her son. Mrs. Anderson was wonderful, thought Meg. She had taken over care of the house soon after Kathy's mother died a year and a half ago, and she had been like a kind grandmother to Kathy.

From where she sat, Meg had a view of the bay. No wonder the house was named Bayview. Looking past Kathy's dark head, she could see the white triangles of two sailboats far out from shore. A little nearer, a shrimp boat poked along, dragging for the brown shrimp that were caught in the small bays behind the offshore islands edging the Gulf Coast.

Suddenly Meg stiffened, every nerve in her body alert. The stranger was back, only now he was standing boldly at the foot of the driveway staring at the group on the terrace.

"Kathy!" she exclaimed, pointing toward the man. "There he is again! And he was on the seawall when I was out this morning, too."

Kathy turned around and took a quick look. "You're right. That's Heron. But I don't see Toad."

Mr. Young touched Kathy's hand. "Heron?" he asked.

"We just call him that," explained Kathy. "Look at him, Dad. Doesn't he look like a heron?"

The man had turned sideways, gazing up the road. In profile he was even more birdlike.

"He has the legs for it. And, yes, that pointed visor looks like a beak." Mr. Young grinned. "You two. You have a gift for names."

Kathy looked puzzled, so Meg repeated what Dan Young had said, using a combination of sign language and finger spelling.

"Do you know him?" Kathy's father asked. "And who is Toad?"

This time Kathy understood. "Toad's a woman who is with him a lot of the time. We don't know either of them. We just see them walking around," she said lightly. "Giving them names, that was just for fun. You know, our people game."

Meg was ready to explode. What was the matter with Kathy? Sure, watching Heron and Toad had started out as a game, but it had become positively scary.

She opened her mouth to tell Kathy's father how the two people had shown up every day last week when she and Kathy walked to and from school, and once had followed them all the way to the door of the junior high. But Kathy put her finger to her lips, signaling for quiet.

Mr. Young's eyes were still on the man who was now standing on the long pier that reached into the bay. "If he and his friend are hanging around, I'd better find out who they are."

"They're tourists," said Mrs. Prentice in her abrupt way. "They stay up the road at the Starfish Cabins. My daughter Essie met them at a fish supper at the community hall."

"Oh, is that so?" Mr. Young looked less worried.

Meg could guess why Kathy didn't want her to say anything about Heron and Toad that would upset her father. But why was Mrs. Prentice trying to make them sound so innocent? Meg was convinced they weren't ordinary tourists. At this distance she couldn't make out Heron's face, but the memory of his intense stare made her shudder.

With difficulty she kept silent, and no more was said about the man.

Mr. Young left for his office in the city of Brighton, thirty miles to the south, and, after helping Mrs. Prentice clear the table, the two girls ran upstairs to Kathy's room, which they were sharing.

Last Friday school had closed for summer vacation, and on Sunday Meg's parents had gone on a two-week trip to Switzerland, leaving their daughter at Bayview with Kathy and her father.

Kathy shut the door to the hall, then leaned

against it, laughing. "One more word and you'd have had Dad calling the police."

"Maybe he should." Meg pronounced each word carefully as she had learned to do when talking with her friend.

Kathy shook her head. "I don't like the way Heron and Toad are always staring at us, but they *could* be a couple of tourists with nothing to do. Whoever they are, I don't want to worry Dad. You know, ever since we — lost Mom — and I got sick, he's always afraid something will happen to me."

Meg dropped onto the twin bed where she had slept the night before. All too clearly she remembered how, two months after Mrs. Young's death, Kathy had had a serious illness that took away most of her hearing. Mr. Young, reeling under all of these blows, had walked around like a man in a daze.

As for Kathy, for a while she had lost interest in everything. Her dark eyes had had a haunted expression. That was when Meg invented the game of looking at people, making up names for them as well as stories about their lives. The imagining had helped Kathy to come through her own deep trouble.

"All right," Meg agreed. "We won't tell your father. I wish I'd talked to Mom and Dad before they went away, but Heron and Toad didn't seem so important last week."

"Yeah," Kathy said slowly. "I'd feel better, too, if we could tell someone about them."

"I wonder what Julian would say," mused Meg.

"That's it! Let's tell him." Kathy jumped up and started to make her bed.

Kathy's back was turned, so Meg reached over and touched her arm to get her attention. "He'll be out on the shrimp boat all morning," she reminded her friend. "Let's go to the wharf right after lunch."

Thinking about Julian, already she felt less worried.

A Visit to Julian

Meg and Kathy had met Julian Benito one Saturday the past January when they were walking along the Oak Point village wharf about a mile from Bayview. January was closed season for bay shrimping, so several boats were moored there.

The two girls had been drawing near to one of the smallest shrimp boats, the *Small Fry*, when a sassy voice called out, "Where are you dolls going?"

Meg's face had felt warm. She wasn't accustomed to being called a doll. Kathy, with her expressive face and splendid dark hair, was the one who usually got the attention. Whoever was talking must be looking only at her.

Meg, who was thin and erect as a fence

post, and had straight light-brown hair and gray eyes, often felt invisible when she was with Kathy. But she didn't mind. Being center stage wasn't important to her.

"She even blushes!" said the male voice.

He *had* noticed her, too, thought Meg. Kathy, of course, hadn't heard the boy, so she hadn't blushed, and if she had, it wouldn't show much because of her olive skin.

Meg faced Kathy and said, "Someone's giving us a line."

Now they were opposite the *Small Fry* and Meg could see the boy sitting cross-legged on the deck, painting the inside of the low rail. He had black hair and looked Spanish, like Kathy, and his dark eyes were friendly.

Meg recognized him at once as a student she had seen at basketball games, but since he was in high school she wouldn't expect him to pay any attention to two girls from junior high. Yet, here he was, smiling at them.

"This is a boring job," he said, speaking slowly. "Stick around and talk to me."

"Why?" demanded Kathy pertly. "Maybe we have something better to do."

But they had stayed and had gotten well acquainted with the talkative Julian. They found out that after school and on Saturday he helped his parents with their shrimp business. Whenever he could, he went out shrimping with his father. His mother sold their catch in a tiny store next to the dock.

"Besides, I get a little spending money gathering news for the radio station." He rubbed his thumb and finger together in an expressive gesture. "You know, school news, sports, anything I can find out."

He was ambitious, that was sure.

One memorable day he and his father had taken the two girls fishing. They'd left the dock before sunrise and stayed out three hours. Dressed in their oldest dungarees and pullovers, they had even helped to cull the trash fish dragged in by the net along with the shrimp.

When Meg and Kathy rode onto the wharf on their bicycles that hot June afternoon, the little shrimp boat was in and Julian was aboard, repairing a net.

"We have a problem for you," said Meg.

"Great. Just what I need, another problem. We hooked onto something on the bottom of the bay and ripped a big hole in our net and lost half our catch. Now what's *your* problem?" Julian made a sweeping motion of welcome toward the freshly scrubbed deck. "Come aboard."

Meg and Kathy took turns telling about Heron and his chubby girl friend, Toad.

"So we're afraid they're up to something. Especially Heron," finished Meg. "What d'you think we ought to do?"

Julian answered promptly, taking care to face Kathy so she could read his lips. "Nothing. You could get into hot water yourselves and make trouble for some innocent people if you go spreading ideas about them."

Meg was disappointed. Julian didn't seem to understand. "You're the only one we've told," she said, "except we just mentioned them to Kathy's father and Mrs. Prentice."

"Sure — and Mrs. Prentice will tell her mousy daughter Essie, and Essie works in the sheriff's office. Next thing, the police will be checking up on your stories."

Meg sputtered, "This isn't a story. You ought to see Heron and that woman. Then you'd know what we mean."

Julian shrugged. "If you don't like these people looking at you, stay away from them."

"It isn't that easy —" began Meg.

"Look!" Kathy interrupted. "There she is now."

"Who?" asked Julian.

"Toad," said Meg excitedly. "She's coming this way. Kathy, you and I ought to turn our backs to her, but Julian, you get a good look. We'll keep on talking and pretend we don't know she's around."

Julian was a born actor. Meg, watching his face, noted how his eyes, half-hidden by his thick lashes, followed the approaching woman while he appeared to be giving all his attention to the torn net.

As soon as Toad had gone past, he grinned at the girls.

"Well?" asked Meg.

"Just a roly-poly little woman," he said. But then he added more seriously, "She did seem to look us over rather thoroughly."

"You see!" Meg said triumphantly.

"It's nothing to get excited about. She was just admiring me," he teased.

Meg was crestfallen. It wasn't like Julian to laugh at the confidences she and Kathy shared with him. She had hoped he'd give them some sensible advice. Today he made her sharply aware that this fall he would be a lordly senior and that he was at least three years older than she.

As they pedaled back along Shore Road toward Bayview, Kathy said, "I guess we're getting too old for this kid stuff about spies and bank robbers."

Meg gave her a quick, amazed glance, then stared down at the twirling wheel of her bicycle to sort out her thoughts.

Apparently she was the only one who

sensed danger. Was it because she wanted to protect Kathy? That she felt responsible for her? No, it was more than that. She had a deep-down distrust of Heron and Toad.

"How'd you like to run into Heron on a dark street?" she asked.

"I wouldn't. But I'm not going on any dark streets, at least not alone."

"Me, either. Let's stick together." Meg left it at that, but she didn't feel satisfied. If Kathy's father knew the two strangers were shadowing them, she was sure he would be concerned.

Kidnapped!

The mile and a half ride home from the town of Oak Point seemed endless. Even the breeze from the bay, tossing their hair and singing in the bicycle wheels, carried little relief from the steamy heat.

When they reached the house Meg collapsed onto her bed. "I'm going to die!" she complained.

Kathy sat down beside her, twisting her heavy hair into a knot on top of her head. "I know. Let's go swimming." She expertly thrust a hairpin into the black knob.

Meg groaned. "I forgot my bathing suit, and I can't bear to go clear home after it. We went right past my house and I never thought of it. What a dope I am!"

"Yeah," Kathy agreed, smiling at her. "You can use one of my suits."

"It won't fit," objected Meg. "I'm taller than you, and skinnier." She motioned as she spoke.

"So what?" demanded Kathy. She tossed a two-piece yellow suit at her friend. "I'll give you some safety pins."

As she and Kathy walked toward the back yard, Meg was self-consciously aware of the lumpy tucks in her bra and pants. "I hope no one sees me like this."

"No one will," Kathy assured her. And it did seem unlikely she'd be seen behind the high oleander hedge that sheltered the pool on three sides.

The soothing coolness of the water made her forget everything but how wonderful it felt. She floated blissfully, reveling in the knowledge that this was fresh water and her hair wouldn't be sticky afterward. She had a fleeting wish for a pool at home, then reminded herself that it didn't really matter. She could always use Kathy's.

If it weren't for Mrs. Prentice, she would feel as much at home at the Young house as she did in her own home half a mile down the road. She and Kathy had been friends ever since kindergarten.

When Kathy had lost her hearing, Mr. Young hired a special teacher for the deaf.

Meg remembered the first day she had met Miss Flora Ryan. The teacher had been trying without much success to interest Kathy in sign language, but soon after Meg arrived the two girls were laughing and making signs to each other. That night Mr. Young had come down to the Carberry house to ask Meg's parents if she could stay with him and Kathy for a while and study with Flora Ryan.

For six happy months, Meg and Kathy had lived and worked together.

After dinner that night Kathy and Meg cleared the table and stacked the dishes in the dishwasher. Mrs. Prentice had a date to go to the movies. She was a widow and two or three times a week went out with a man she referred to only as "my friend." He always pulled up to the front terrace in an ancient green two-door and sat there waiting, smoking or combing his thick pepper-and-salt hair. Sometimes he tooted the horn, but he never got out of the car or rang the doorbell.

As soon as the dishes were in the dishwasher, Kathy headed for the television to watch a program, an interview with an artist.

Meg roamed around the living room. She wasn't interested in the interview. Kathy was the one who wanted to be an artist. As for herself, she wanted to be like Flora Ryan and teach deaf children.

Mr. Young was across the room reading the newspaper. One hand absent-mindedly caressed Rusty's head.

The dog's eyes followed Meg as she wandered around the big room. Soon he scrambled to his feet and, coming across to her, rubbed his head against her legs.

"Right," said Meg. "We need a walk." She sat down on the davenport beside Kathy and caught her attention. "I'm going home after my bathing suit," she said. Tomorrow Kathy's father was taking the two girls to a nearby island for a swim and lunch. She wouldn't be caught dead wearing a pinned-on suit in public.

Mr. Young looked up from his paper. "Want a ride?"

"No. Thanks, though. Rusty and I like to prowl along the shore."

She snapped on the dog's leash, then touched Kathy on the shoulder and waved good-bye.

Kathy lifted one hand. " 'Bye. Y'all come back." This was one of their private jokes. Every store clerk used the same expression.

As soon as she was outside, Meg let out the rope she had fastened to the end of the leash. Rusty, exuberant, raced down the circular drive and, with some urging, turned south on Shore Road.

The sun was now in the west and they were cooled by the long shadows cast by the live oak trees on the landward side of the road.

Rusty's riotous approach sent small, quick-legged birds scurrying across the sand. The herons and white egrets that stalked the shallow water paid little attention to him.

Meg checked to see if the tall stranger with the baseball cap were in sight, but the shore and road were deserted except for a van far ahead, parked on the hard-packed sand. A man was in the water, casting for fish. People frequently went wade-fishing along here. For the past week or so it seemed someone was always tossing out a line.

Only one house stood in the half-mile stretch of road between Youngs' and Carberrys'. That was an ancient landmark called the Ogden house.

Meg walked past slowly, studying it while Rusty pulled on his leash. She was fascinated by the gloomy-looking mansion with the tower topped by a widow's walk. Once it had been a beautiful place and people had paid to go through it. Although for years it had stood empty, it still drew the curious and the mischievous like a magnet. Meg and Kathy had prowled through the house one afternoon a month ago and had come away sickened at the way vandals had smashed the plaster cupids that decorated the archways and had written their names on the white walls.

Meg was almost past the house when she saw an old blue panel truck pull into the rear driveway. She paused and watched a tall young man with red hair and beard get out of the truck and go toward the house carrying what looked like a toolbox. She had heard a rumor that someone had bought the house and was going to fix it up. It must be true. The man opened the back door and went inside.

Just past the Ogden house was the fisherman's van she had noticed when she started out, a brown one such as many people used for traveling. The window in the second door on the side facing her was curtained with brown-and-yellow material, but beyond that, the rear wall of the van was solid. The fisherman was still in the water nearby, faded dungarees rolled up to his knees. His back was toward Meg but she could see that he had shoulder-length brown hair.

Rusty would have splashed out to greet him if Meg had not held him back.

"Any luck?" she called.

The man didn't turn around, but he answered something that sounded like, "Not even a bite!"

The Carberry house had a closed-up, lonely look. Meg tied the dog to the porch railing, then ran inside. She scurried around, watering the plants, then went upstairs for her bathing suit.

In her room she lingered at the window overlooking the bay, feeling a little homesick. This house was closer to the road than Bayview and was located on a slight rise, giving a long view of the water and of the shore to the north and south.

She watched idly while the lone fisherman almost a quarter of a mile up the road walked onto the beach and climbed into the van.

Meg tucked her bathing suit into a plastic bag and ran downstairs. Outside, she untied Rusty and started back toward the Youngs'.

The part of Shore Road that lay between the Young and Carberry houses was almost straight, so Meg could see a figure, far ahead and dwarfed by distance, walking toward her on the shore side of the road. Even at that distance Meg was sure she recognized Kathy's vigorous stride. Her friend must have decided to come to meet her.

Meg began to hurry, trying to pace herself so they'd meet at the halfway point, a large live oak near the Ogden house. Now she could see Kathy's long hair blowing back in the wind, but the coral of her shirt was still grayed by distance.

The fisherman's van was heading north but moving so slowly it was only a short distance from the old house.

Rusty pulled toward the beach, and Meg let him tow her across the road. She could see Kathy better on this side, anyway.

The van was approaching Kathy, but she was striding along with her head turned toward the bay.

The taillights of the vehicle blinked on. It must be stopping. Meg stared earnestly ahead, trying to see more clearly. She walked faster, although her chest hurt already from her rapid pace.

It was automatic for her to keep track of Kathy.

I'm like Kathy's father, she thought. Both of us think she can't get along without us.

Now she was sure the van was standing still. A shaggy head poked out the window on the side toward the bay. That must be the fisherman. Probably he had slid across the seat to ask Kathy a question.

Meg saw her friend turn her head and then step closer to the van. Probably she couldn't hear what the driver was saying and was trying to read his lips. He must be a tourist asking for directions.

Rusty whimpered and pulled forward. Meg

bent and unsnapped the leash from his collar, saying, "Go see Kathy!" But the command was unnecessary. Already the dog was racing up the road, reaching out with his gangly young legs.

Meg kept her eyes on the van, far ahead.

The door behind the driver opened slightly and Kathy stepped back as if to talk to someone in the rear seat. Why would she have to give directions to a passenger in the back?

Next, to Meg's surprise, the driver got out and pulled the rear door open wider. He stood directly behind Kathy.

Meg felt a prickle run up the back of her neck, a forewarning of danger. Something was wrong. The whole thing was like a tense moment in a TV movie when the sound went dead. She wasn't close enough to hear a single word. Wondering if this was what it was like to be deaf, Meg began to run toward the van. She thought she heard Rusty's bark. He had already covered more than half the distance.

Suddenly the scene ahead changed dramatically. Kathy turned her head toward the driver and began to back away. At that the man gave her a strong push toward the open door.

Meg screamed, but there was no sign that she was heard. Even while she ran as fast as she could go, she kept her eyes on her friend. Kathy was trying to pull away, but she didn't have a chance.

Rusty, still traveling toward her, wasn't close enough to help.

To Meg's horror, she saw Kathy disappear into the van. The sound of the door slamming shut came back as a faint thud, muffled by the cries of the gulls and the wind in the salt grass.

The van leaped forward and sped away as if it were drag racing.

Within seconds the road ahead was empty except for the dog, running steadily in the direction taken by the van.

The Hooded Man

As soon as the TV interview with the artist was over, Kathy started down the road to meet Meg.

It was a warm night and the breeze from the bay felt good. It lifted her hair, cooling the back of her neck where her black mane was heaviest.

Kathy loved wind. It was so alive it made her feel like running and becoming a part of it. She wished she could make great leaps the way ballet dancers did.

The sun, though hidden from her by the trees on her right, still shone on the bay. A trick of the light made the troughs of the waves royal blue while the tops were green. It would be interesting to paint the same scene at several different times of day. There were so many pictures she wanted to make. She was going to be an artist, at least she hoped so. Her art teacher at school said she was good.

She thought wistfully about the summer art workshop she had been invited to attend. It really would be great to live for a month in a dormitory with other art students her age and take classes in sketching and painting and design.

It was the chance of a lifetime — but she just couldn't go, not without Meg. The college where the workshop was to be held was in Brighton, thirty miles south of Oak Point. Her father's office was in that city so she could see him now and then. But no one she knew would be at the school. No one there would know sign language or finger spelling. What if she didn't understand the teacher? Who would explain to her? And how would the other students feel about a person who was deaf?

Kathy felt uneasy at the idea of being on her own. Dad said the workshop was a big opportunity, but he wouldn't tell her what to do. He said it was her decision.

Dad tried so hard to be a father and a mother, and he was great. The best dad ever. But Kathy often thought how wonderful it would be to have a woman in the house she could talk to.

Mrs. Prentice was no help that way. In fact, Kathy liked the nights when the housekeeper went out. Even though Mrs. Prentice usually went to her room when she had cleaned up the kitchen after dinner, her unsmiling presence seemed to darken the entire house.

She wasn't like their former housekeeper, Mrs. Anderson, or Flora Ryan, the teacher who had helped her to cope after she became deaf. Dear Flora, she had been such fun, playing Scrabble with them all in the evening, sitting around the fire on cool winter evenings, toasting marshmallows, and talking, talking.

Mrs. Anderson had often joined them, and they had been like a real family.

All too soon Flora had said that Kathy could manage without her. That she knew sign language and finger spelling and could read lips fairly well. All Kathy needed now was practice, and she could do that with Meg. As for Mr. Young, the two girls could help him improve his ability to talk with his hands and to practice enunciating more clearly so it would be easier to read his lips.

Flora was getting married. She had kept her fiancé waiting until she was sure Kathy was ready to be on her own. In a short time she was far away in North Dakota.

Kathy had missed her, but even so it hadn't been too bad until Mrs. Anderson left. Right away Mrs. Prentice applied for the job and Dad had decided to hire her on a trial basis. Neither he nor Kathy was happy with her, but Dad hadn't yet found anyone to take her place.

Kathy was so deep in thought she was startled when she looked to her right and saw that a car had stopped close beside her. It was a dark brown van.

The driver had slid over to the passenger side and was leaning out the window. His lips were moving but, though Kathy could hear a mumble, with the wind and the gulls' cries she couldn't understand what he was saying.

She moved closer to the van. "What do you want?"

Again he spoke, and this time she was able to catch the word Galveston. He must want to go there.

"Keep going north about half a mile, then turn left," she began.

The man lifted his hand and interrupted her. He pointed to the back seat. "Talk to my friend back there. He's the navigator."

This time Kathy was able to read his words. But why should she explain to someone else? Couldn't the driver remember a few simple directions? A yellow-and-brown striped curtain covered the tightly closed second window. She wondered how she was supposed to communicate with the person back there out of sight.

Then she noticed that the back door was ajar. Obediently she moved to talk through the opening. It was dark inside the van, and she could see only a dim figure on the seat.

"Go straight ahead —" she began again.

The car door opened wider, and Kathy looked back to see who had moved it. To her surprise, the driver stood behind her with one hand still on the door.

She didn't like his closeness. There was no reason for him to get out of the car. She became aware of the emptiness of the road. There was only one way to escape and that was back and to her right.

Her quick leap in that direction was too late.

The driver reached out and shoved her toward the open door. As she staggered, off balance, a strong arm shot out from the back seat and seized her wrist.

Kathy screamed and fought with all her strength, but the grip was like iron. The man behind her put his hands on either side of her waist and lifted her into the back seat.

As she tumbled forward, she had a glimpse of a dark hood with two round holes through which a pair of eyes shone wickedly.

Again Kathy screamed.

A hand covered her mouth, smothering her cries. At the same time she felt the stab of a needle in her right hip.

The door slammed shut, the driver slid into the front seat, and then the van took off with a bound.

At first Kathy struggled to break free. But soon she felt drowsy and nothing seemed to matter. It reminded her of the time when she had had her tonsils removed. Her mind began to play tricks on her, and she imagined she was again in the operating room. The hooded man was a doctor. He's going to be surprised, she thought fuzzily, when he finds out I haven't any tonsils.

Seconds later she lost the last shred of consciousness.

Captive Afloat

Kathy's nose was the first part of her to signal her brain when she awakened from her drugged sleep. It picked up the scents of fresh air, fish, and tar.

Next she felt a rocking sensation. It was a gentle motion, like being in a boat on a day when there was little wind.

She could hear no sound, but that was not unusual. She always took off her hearing aid when she went to bed. But she didn't remember removing it last night.

Last night! What had happened?

Wide awake now, she opened her eyes to darkness. Turning her head, she could see the sky through an open doorway. The stars rose and fell with the rocking motion. She must be on a boat. How had she gotten here?

Memories rushed into her brain. That van. And that hooded person. It all came back to her.

I've been kidnapped!

The driver had picked her up and thrust her into the van. She remembered falling forward and the sharp pain as someone had stabbed her with a needle. Then everything had gone blank.

While she was unconscious they must have carried her onto this boat. She couldn't feel the vibration of the engine so it wasn't traveling anywhere now.

Why were they hiding her on a boat? Her stomach turned to lead as she thought. Perhaps because it would be easy to toss her overboard if she got in the way?

Kathy hastily pushed aside that idea. If she gave way to fear she wouldn't be able to think. This was something she had learned during those bewildering days when she had first lost her hearing.

One morning when she had burst into tears of frustration at not being able to understand what was being said, Flora Ryan, her teacher, had written, "Keep calm. It does no good to panic. That just scrambles your brains."

Now, more than ever before, she needed to think clearly.

First, who was on this boat with her? If only she could hear, she might be able to pick up voices or movement. She lifted her hand to her ear and then to the placket of her shirt, hoping to find her hearing aid and to adjust it.

To her dismay, the body aid was not clipped to her shirt. The earpiece was still in her ear, but that was all that was left. Besides, the shirt she was wearing wasn't her own. Someone had removed her coral blouse and had replaced it with a too large shirt that buttoned like a boy's. She took out the earpiece and tucked it into the pocket of her jeans.

Something else was wrong, but in her concern over the disappearance of her hearing aid, the other loss hadn't registered.

When she raised her hand to her head again, she recognized what was missing. Her long hair had been chopped off. Whoever had done it had been no expert with the shears. She could feel the stubby ends. She must be a sight. But she had more important things to think about.

Where was her hearing aid? Without moving from the place where she lay, she felt on all sides in the hope of finding it nearby, but her fingers only touched rough rope, slightly sticky. It felt like a net. That was it — she was on a pile of fishing nets, shrimp nets, probably. That explained the tarry smell and the stickiness. She knew the fishermen dipped their nets in tar to shed unwanted fish and slime and prevent rotting.

She remembered when Julian and his father had taken Meg and her out for a day's shrimping. From what little she could see in the moonlight, this appeared to be the same kind of boat. She must be in the pilothouse. Outside the door was the deck, open to the sky.

At night the bay shrimpers kept their boats tied to a dock or floating at anchor. There were strict rules they had to follow. According to regulations, they couldn't start fishing until thirty minutes before sunrise.

If this boat were at a dock, she should be able to escape.

Sitting up straight on the nets, Kathy looked all around the pilothouse. As far as she could tell, no one else was there. She might even be the only person on the boat. Perhaps they thought the drug would keep her asleep longer than it had.

But before she explored the rest of the boat, she wanted to find her hearing aid. She longed to pick up sounds, the creaking of the boat lifted by the waves, the cry of gulls, any voise that would make her feel a part of the place where she was. And if there were other people on the boat, she wanted to be able to hear them when they spoke.

She got onto her knees and crawled all over the pile of nets without finding anything.

Next she explored the small pilothouse, first the floor, then the tops of the built-in storage boxes below the windows, and, finally, the narrow window ledges. She found no hearing aid, and, in her quick glances through the windows, she saw no sign of land.

Finally, she had to give up, knowing she was wasting precious time.

Silently she crept toward the open door. Straight ahead the deck lay empty. She looked cautiously to the right. No one. Then to the left. The moon, low in the western sky, showed her a dark hump against the wall of the pilothouse. Two legs — no, four — stretched out from the hump.

Disappointed, Kathy drew her head back. Those two people might be asleep, but she couldn't be sure. She must plan her move, for she might not get another chance as good as this.

She could swim, but she couldn't keep going for a long time. If the boat were at a dock or anchored near shore, she'd be all right. But if they were far from land or the tide was running out, she knew she wouldn't make it.

Through the door that opened onto the deck she could see nothing but water, reflecting the light of the moon.

With great care she again skirted the pile of nets and went from window to window for a more thorough look. Not a boat was in sight, but, when she had stared through the pilot's window for several minutes, she picked out the dark line of the land, far across the water. A few faint lights showed here and there. Twice the twin gleam of a car's headlights moved along parallel to the shore.

Land was a long way off. She was aware that probably it was even farther than it seemed. But she thought she could reach it. She could swim and float, turn about. If only she could locate a life jacket, that would be even better.

She could wake up the sleeping kidnappers and say, "Where are the life preservers? I want to escape."

Funny, funny, Meg would say.

She wished Meg were there. No. It was better to have her free. Perhaps she had seen the van that picked her up and could identify it. Kathy hadn't seen Meg on the road, but then, she had been lost in her own thoughts and hadn't looked ahead.

Poor Dad! she thought. He'll be so worried. I suppose they'll ask him for money. I hope it isn't a lot.

Thinking of her father brought tears to her eyes. If only she could get away, he wouldn't have to pay any ransom.

Kathy put everything out of her mind except escape plans.

The only door in the pilothouse was the one that led to the deck, in plain view of the two people who were sitting out there. The windows in the little cabin did not open. That meant her only escape route lay through the door to the deck. She would have to be quick and silent.

Sitting down on the nets, she removed her sneakers. They would be too heavy for swimming. Once in the water, she'd pull off the jeans, too.

Barefooted, she padded to the doorway and peered out. The two people were still beside the wall of the pilothouse. She hoped they were asleep.

Here goes! she thought, crossing her fingers for luck.

She drew a deep breath and walked swiftly out the door, turned right, and reached the narrow strip of deck between the rail and the pilothouse, out of sight of the kidnappers. The distant lights beckoned her. She leaned down and put one leg over the low rail, dreading the plunge into the dark, unknown water. But there was no other way to escape.

Bending over farther, she got a firm grip on the rail, ready to climb over the rest of the way.

Something cold pressed against the back of her neck, bringing her to a sudden halt.

She couldn't hear a sound, but she was sure the cold object was the muzzle of a gun, and its steady pressure spoke more clearly than any words.

Nightmare

Kathy had been kidnapped!

Panting for breath, Meg stared up the road, unable to believe what she had seen. Kathy and the van had disappeared as if by magic. But Rusty was a bouncing dot far down the road, still pursuing the out-of-sight van.

There was no doubt about it. Kathy hadn't wanted to get into that van. She had pulled back and tried to get away.

Although she was still breathing heavily, Meg again ran up the road. Her thoughts were in a turmoil. What was happening to Kathy? Would the people in the van hurt her? No doubt they wanted money. They must think Mr. Young was wealthy. Probably he was. Meg had never given it much thought, but she knew oil had been discovered on the property that had come down to him from his cattle-raising grandfather. His ancestors had been early settlers in southeastern Texas.

Meg passed the place where the van had stopped. The tires had left black streaks on the pavement when the kidnappers made their fast getaway.

She staggered up the driveway and across the terrace to the door. Through the window she could see Kathy's father look up from the paper he was reading. Something about her appearance must have startled him, for he leaped to his feet and met her at the door.

"What's the — ?" he began.

Meg interrupted him. "Kathy . . ." It was all she could say. She pointed to the road.

Mr. Young looked terrified. He rushed to the door, then back. "Where is she? What happened?"

Meg gulped in great lungsful of air. "A van. It stopped — and took her away."

"Someone she knew?"

Meg shook her head. "No." It was becoming easier to breathe but she couldn't control the trembling of her voice. "I was way down the road, but I saw her kick and try to get away. Someone pulled her in. I sent Rusty to her but he didn't get there in time."

Dan rushed to the phone and began to dial. He called to Meg. "I'm getting the sheriff. Come here. Describe the van." He spoke into the phone. "Sheriff Weaver, please. Hurry. This is an emergency."

Meg dropped onto the chair beside the phone table, trying to recall exactly what she had seen. She knew Sheriff Weaver. Everyone in the county knew the heavy-set, friendly man, and her father was a special friend of his. Several times he had been to their house for dinner. And how he liked to eat!

Now Mr. Young was talking to him. In a moment he handed her the phone. No matter how unhappy and confused she felt, she had to hang onto her self-control to help Kathy.

The sheriff's questions came at her like gun-fire but she answered them as well as she could. "When? Just a few minutes ago," she told him. "I came right here and Mr. Young called you."

"What kind of car?" he asked.

"A van," she said. "Brown. Two doors on the side. . . . Curtains in the windows. I didn't see the driver's face, but he had long hair to his shoulders. Brown. The license? It was Texas. I didn't notice the numbers. . . . Kathy had on dungarees and a coral shirt."

When she had told the sheriff all she could, she handed the phone back to Mr. Young.

He said briefly, "Thanks, sheriff. If you will, please. Yes. We'll be here."

After he had hung up, he said, "The sheriff is sending out a message to all police units. The news will blanket the area in five minutes. Thank heaven you saw what happened. And that you came right here."

He put his arm around her shoulders. "What are we going to *do*, Meg?" His voice trembled.

It was strange to have him ask her for help. He walked away and stood in front of the open door with his hands braced on either side of the frame. His back was toward Meg, but she could see his shoulders shaking.

Tears poured down Meg's face.

Soon Kathy's father straightened and faced her. He seemed calm, though his face was haggard. "Where's Rusty?" he asked.

"He was still running after the van, last I saw him." She rubbed her eyes on her sleeve.

Dan Young pulled a clean handkerchief from his pocket and gave it to her. "Meg, we'll get her back," he said reassuringly. "We *have* to." He pushed the screen open. "Let's go out and see if Rusty's around." He paused. "No. Will you stay here in case the phone rings? I'll be right back."

Meg stood on the terrace and watched him go down the driveway at a fast jog. When he reached the road, he looked to the north, then to the south. She heard him whistle for the dog.

This was a nightmare, and she'd soon wake up. Not Kathy! She couldn't be gone. Any minute the van would come up the driveway and she'd jump out and say, "Surprise! I'm back."

When Dan returned he said, "No sign of Rusty." He slumped into a chair. "Are you *sure* there wasn't some friend of Kathy's in that van?"

Meg nodded. "At least I know she didn't want to go with them." She hesitated. "You know that man we saw this morning? We call him Heron."

Dan Young's eyes bored into hers. "Yes. What about him?"

Briefly Meg wondered if she should say more about the two strangers. Julian had said the girls could get into trouble, accusing someone when they had no evidence. But she *had* to tell anything that might help. "Well, we — I — thought he — Heron — was following us around. He never did anything and he didn't talk to us, but he kept showing up all the time."

"Why didn't you tell me?"

"We — didn't want to worry you for nothing."

He stared at her. "This morning. You were going to say something about him, weren't you? But Kathy and Mrs. Prentice put you off."

Meg was mute. She didn't want to get her friend into trouble with her father.

Footsteps sounded on the terrace. Mr. Young jumped up. "That'll be Weaver." He flung open the screen door. Even before the sheriff was inside, he said excitedly, "Meg has a suspect. Come in. Sit down."

Sheriff Weaver dropped heavily into a comfortable chair facing Meg and Mr. Young on the davenport. He took out a notebook and pen. "Tell me about it."

"We — Kathy and I — noticed two people," said Meg, "a man and a woman. We don't know their names but we called them Heron and Toad because of the way they looked."

The men were giving her all their attention. Encouraged by the interest, she went on to describe the two strangers.

"Where do they come from?" asked the sheriff.

"We think they're staying at the Starfish Cabins."

Dan Young interrupted. "That's what Essie said, according to Mrs. Prentice."

Weaver said, "Mrs. La Rose's cabins. Nice woman. I'll give her a call."

Meg waited tensely while the sheriff talked to the owner of the Starfish Cabins. He didn't seem to think it was silly to be concerned about Heron and Toad. She wished she had told Mr. Young about them this morning. If she had, maybe Kathy wouldn't have been kidnapped.

Heron hadn't been driving the van, though. She had seen the long-haired young man climb into the driver's seat. But Heron might have been inside. Probably he was the one Kathy had talked to through the doorway. The more she thought about it, the more convinced she was that he was guilty. He must have been on the watch, waiting for a chance to get Kathy alone.

The sheriff put down the phone and came across the room, shaking his head.

"We'll have to scratch your suspects, Meg. They've both been playing bridge with Mrs. La Rose all evening."

Meg was stunned. She groped for an explanation. "Maybe they're not the right people. I mean, maybe they're not Heron and Toad."

"Mrs. La Rose says your description is perfect for two of the people at her cabins. Heron she's sure is Sidney Tripp. Tall, thin, with round shoulders. Always wears a baseball cap with a long visor."

Meg nodded mutely. It was a perfect description of Heron.

"He's a widower," Sheriff Weaver went on. "Mrs. La Rose thinks he's looking for a new wife. He's been dating a Miss Morgan. Her first name's Ann. That would be your Toad. A short, chunky woman with curly brown hair. Often wears a brown blouse and slacks. Very alert. Looks around a lot and doesn't miss a thing."

"That's Toad, all right," agreed Meg.

"Interesting thing about her," the sheriff went on. "She's a private detective from up north someplace. You were right about her, Meg. No doubt she was watching you and Kathy. She has the habit of keeping an eye on people."

Meg's spirits sank still lower. If Heron and Toad were innocent, who had taken Kathy away?

A Click on the Line

"Dan," said Sheriff Weaver, "you'll probably hear from the people who picked up Kathy." He paused. "I'm assuming this is a kidnapping. You're well known, and someone has figured out you'd pay a lot to get your daughter back."

Mr. Young drew in a deep breath, then nodded.

"If you do get a message," the sheriff went on, "let me know."

"Right."

"What about ransom?" asked Weaver. "Would you pay it?"

"Anything to get Kathy back," Dan Young said firmly.

"I'd feel the same way," said Weaver. "Now if word gets out that ransom is to be delivered, there could be reporters hiding behind trees to catch the action. And that might blow it. So don't talk to anyone but me."

"There's bound to be publicity about her disappearance."

"Sure, but I'd say that's good. People will be watching for her and the van. Might help. By the way, where's that photo you said you'd give me?"

Kathy's father reached for a picture that lay on the end table beside him. "This is the latest one I have."

Weaver studied it. "Beautiful. I'll get this back to you."

"Then it's all right for me to talk about what happened so far?" asked Meg.

"Well, that depends on who you talk to and how much information you give out."

"Kathy and I have a friend — Julian Benito. He's in high school. I'd like to tell him. He'd help look for Kathy and the van."

"Sure. I know him," said the sheriff. "Go ahead."

Meg recalled something else about Julian. "He's a reporter for the radio station in Oak Point. He might want to call in the story."

"That should be all right. Give him the full description of the van and what Kathy was wearing. Everything you told us. But warn him not to mention your name. And don't let him say anything about those two you suspected. You could get in trouble throwing suspicion on innocent people."

Just what Julian said, thought Meg.

Dan Young wearily rubbed his face. "I know we're going to have newsmen camped at our door, and, Sheriff, I think you know what to tell them better than I do. Could Meg and I simply say your office is answering all questions?"

"Sure. But that won't keep some media people from taking pictures and following you around." Weaver gazed at Meg with a worried expression on his broad, tanned face. "There's another thing. Meg shouldn't wander around alone. The people who picked up Kathy may know she saw them."

Meg stared at him, surprised that she hadn't thought of this herself. "I was a long way off, and I think they were too busy with Kathy to look back at me. Anyway, it'll be on the TV and radio and in the newspapers, the description of the van and the man who was driving it. I don't see why they'd try to shut me up after I've already told everything I know."

The sheriff nodded slowly. "You may be right. But be careful, anyway."

"I'll look after her." Mr. Young glanced across at Meg. "I wonder if we should get in touch with your parents."

"Oh, no!" she protested. "They've looked forward to this trip for so long."

"Well, all right. Of course they may hear anyway. News like this travels fast," he said. "But in that case, they'd phone us. Oh, Sheriff, will you have your men on the lookout for Rusty? You know he followed the van, and he hasn't come back yet."

As soon as Sheriff Weaver left, Meg phoned Julian and told him about Kathy's disappearance and her conversation with the sheriff.

"Hey, Meg, I'm sorry," he said. "I'll find out if any of the shrimpers have seen her or if they've noticed anyone acting suspicious. Is there anything else I can do?"

"Keep watch for Rusty. And, oh! You can phone the radio station."

"Thanks! I forgot I'm a reporter. Would it help to have it on radio?"

"It might. But don't mention I'm the one who saw Kathy picked up."

"Of course not. And you be careful. Don't open the door to anyone you don't know."

"Yes, sir!"

"And Meg, I'll keep in touch. Hang in there, now."

When Julian rang off, Meg leaned back in the chair, still holding the receiver. How great it was to have a friend like Julian. His kindness and the concern in his voice had weakened her defenses and she could feel her eyes burning.

She was startled by the sound of a click on the line, as if a phone were being hung up. She glanced into the living room where she could see Mr. Young standing at the door. He hadn't been on the extension, then, and Julian had cut off moments ago. This was not a party line. Who had been listening in on the conversation?

She replaced the receiver and went into the living room. "Who could be listening in on our phone, do you think? I just heard someone hang up after Julian and I got through talking."

Kathy's father turned around, and she was shocked by how much older his face looked. "Probably Mrs. Prentice. I heard her come in the back door a few minutes ago. She might have tried to make a call and found out the line was in use."

"Oh," said Meg. But that explanation didn't quite ring true. Why hadn't Mrs. Prentice hung up right away when she found the line was busy?

"I'm going out in a little while to look for Rusty," said Mr. Young. "I can't sleep, anyway."

He closed and locked the front door. "Come on. Let's see Mrs. Prentice and tell her what's happened. Then you go to bed. You'd hear the phone even if you were asleep, wouldn't you?"

"I usually do," said Meg.

Mrs. Prentice had a living room, bedroom, and bath in the north wing of the house. When she answered the tap on her door, she was still fully dressed and seemed to have been watching a movie on television.

Dan Young said, "Sit down, Mrs. Prentice. We have some very bad news."

She gave him a quick glance, then dropped into a chair. As soon as he told her about Kathy, she cried out, "Oh, no! What a terrible thing to happen!" She pulled out a handkerchief and dabbed at her eyes. "What can we do?"

That's an act, thought Meg. I'm sure it is. She doesn't look surprised. Must be she heard me tell Julian.

"Have you seen Rusty?" asked Mr. Young.

"No. Isn't he in the yard or his doghouse?"

"He wasn't a while ago, but I'll check again," said Kathy's father. "I'm going out now to look for him. Meg will take any calls for me. She was here when the sheriff came and she knows all the details," he explained.

Mrs. Prentice looked offended. Meg guessed that she would have preferred to be the one to answer the phone.

The woman's face was grim as she said, "Very well."

While undressing, Meg listened to the local radio station. In a short time she heard the announcer say, "We interrupt this program for a news special."

The account of Kathy's abduction was just as she had given it to Julian, and she found that she had become "an unidentified by-stander." People were asked to watch for Kathy and for "a young Chesapeake Bay retriever that answers to the name of Rusty."

At seven the next morning, Dan Young called Meg to the phone. It was Sheriff Weaver.

"Meg, we've found a van that fits the description you gave me. Can you take a look at it?"

"Yes, I have to get dressed. Any word on Rusty?"

"No, not yet. Sorry. I'll pick you up in fifteen minutes."

"What about Mr. Young?" asked Meg. "Isn't he coming too?"

"No. He's staying near the phone in case he gets a call from the kidnappers."

When Meg got out of the sheriff's car at his office, a press photographer lifted his camera. Weaver stepped in front of Meg. "No pictures of her." He waggled his finger at the man. "I know you don't want to put her in danger."

The photographer lowered his camera. "O.K., Sheriff."

The van was in the parking lot where it had been towed by the sheriff's men.

"That looks like it!" said Meg. She walked all the way around the van. Everything about it was like the vehicle she had seen parked beside the road the day before. Even the brown-and-yellow striped curtains were the same.

"We found it outside town on a dirt road," said the sheriff.

"May I get inside?" Meg hoped she might find something of Kathy's, or some clue.

"Sure. We've fingerprinted it already, just in case it was the right one."

There was nothing on the front or back seats or on the floor between them. Meg got onto her hands and knees and ran her hand under the front seats. Then she turned and did the same for the rear one. In the front corner of the right-hand rear seat she felt something like a thick piece of string. She pulled it gently, already sure of what she had found.

On the other end of the cord was the little case Kathy carried in the pocket of her shirt or clipped to the placket. It was the power part of her hearing aid that contained the transistor and the batteries.

Meg showed it to the sheriff. With a voice she couldn't quite control, she said, "It's Kathy's — the battery pack for her hearing aid. May I keep it until she comes back? She can't hear without this little case."

Rusty

When the sheriff returned Meg to Bayview, no cars were in the driveway.

"Good," commented Weaver. "You're certainly not being besieged by the press. I put out a bulletin this morning saying my office would handle all news releases. Maybe it worked."

Just then a Chevette pulled up behind them. Weaver looked back and said with a smile, "My mistake. Here comes a reporter now."

Julian climbed out of the Chevette and hurried to the sheriff's car. "Any news yet?" He leaned his arms, bare to the elbow, against the window frame on the side next to Meg and thrust his head inside to give her a kiss.

Meg flushed with pleasure. It didn't mean anything, she told herself. He was just being friendly, but that was something.

"We have the van," said the sheriff. "Meg just identified it."

"Where'd you find it?"

"About ten miles south of Oak Point, parked in plain sight on the edge of a dirt road. They didn't care if we found it, that's sure."

Julian opened the car door and sat down beside Meg. "I've been talking to the shrimpers and anyone I could find, telling them to be on the lookout for a pretty girl with long black hair. I don't suppose it does any good. Those kidnappers could be five hundred miles away by now."

The sheriff tilted his head to one side, considering. "Might not be. Kathy could be right under our noses."

"I thought of a good place to hide someone," said Meg. "The old Ogden house. It's under our noses. It even has a secret place."

"That closed-up house on Shore Road?" asked Julian. "That'd be a fine spot, I guess, except anybody'd notice if people went in and out of there."

"Vandals have been going in and out for

years and we haven't caught them," Weaver pointed out.

"And did you know there's someone working there now?" demanded Meg.

"No." Julian grinned. "I take it all back. That must be the perfect hideout."

Meg said, "I walked past yesterday when I was on my way home to get my bathing suit, and I saw a man with red hair. He got out of a blue truck."

The sheriff asked, "Did he go into the house?"

"Yes."

Weaver's eyes had a look of intense interest. "It's worth a look. I'll round up some men and make an official call. I'll get a search warrant if I have to, but maybe the redhead will let me in."

"May I go, too?" Meg asked eagerly.

"Wish I could take you. I know what sharp eyes you have. But I don't dare. If your hunch about the old house is right, it could be a dangerous place to visit."

"How much of this can I give out to the radio station?" asked Julian.

"Nothing about the Ogden house until after we check it," said Weaver. "Give me a number where I can reach you and I'll let you know what we find."

"I'm going to be traveling around," said Julian. "I thought Meg and I might do some detective work. Dad has a friend helping him today so I get time off."

"All right." The sheriff leaned forward, talking across Meg. "Let me know if you find any clues. Call me in a couple of hours and we can report to each other. I trust you not to put any news on the air that'll put Kathy in any more danger. And take it easy," he warned. "It could be unhealthy if you get too close to the truth."

"Right," Julian agreed. "I won't spill anything you want kept quiet. Meg and Kathy are like kid sisters to me."

Huh! thought Meg. So I'm a *kid* sister. She didn't want Julian to think of her as a kid *or* a sister.

The sheriff got out of the car. "I'm going in to talk to Dan."

"And I'm starved," said Meg, patting her flat stomach. "I didn't take time for breakfast. Come in with us," she invited Julian.

They were halfway across the terrace when Dan Young pushed open the screen door. His face was even more tense than before. Meg noticed that he was wearing the same shirt as yesterday. Hadn't he gone to bed at all last night?

"I just got a phone call." His voice was like a croak. "So now we know what they want."

"Ransom?" asked the sheriff.

"Right. If I ever want to see Kathy again —" Dan cleared his throat and swallowed hard before he went on. "That's what they said, if I ever want to see her, I'm to deliver five hundred thousand in small bills."

"Did you recognize the voice?" asked Weaver.

"No. It had a weird sound, like a recording being played too slow."

"Half a million," said the sheriff. "Can you get hold of that much?"

"I guess so. The small bills, that'll take a while. I'm going out now and make the rounds of the banks." He turned to Julian. "Don't give out news about the ransom request."

"I won't," Julian promised.

Dan Young started away, then turned back. "Can someone look after Meg?"

"Yes, sir," said Julian. "I plan to."

Meg was both amused and rebellious. I don't need a keeper, she thought.

When she and Julian entered the kitchen, the table in the breakfast alcove had been cleared and Mrs. Prentice was no place in sight.

Meg scouted for food. "How about a Danish?" she asked. "And there's a little coffee left in the pot."

"Great. Where are the cups?"

"Up there." Meg pointed to a cupboard to the right of the sink. "None for me. I'm having milk."

Julian opened the leaded glass door and produced a cup.

As they sat at the kitchen table, he remarked, "Since Kathy's father has gotten that call, the police will be working harder than ever."

Meg set down her glass of milk. "I suppose so. Now they're sure it wasn't a friend who picked her up."

Julian's brown eyes studied the enamel table. "I hear the Texas Rangers are already on the case." He glanced up at Meg. "With all the professionals working, I guess it's crazy to think we could discover anything they can't. But I have this feeling I *have* to do something."

"Me, too." Meg understood exactly what Julian meant. It was impossible to sit still while Kathy was in this awful fix. "What's your plan?"

Julian swallowed the last bite of his Danish. "How about we drive north up the road the way the van headed? Then we stop along the way and ask people if they saw it go by. Maybe someone got a good look at the driver. We ought to go to the Starfish Cabins, too."

Meg jumped to her feet and gathered up her dishes. "Let's get started!" As she walked toward the dishwasher, her eyes caught a flicker of movement reflected in the glass of the cupboard doors. She whirled around just in time to see Mrs. Prentice disappearing into the hall on the far side of the dining room. How long had she been in there? The door between the kitchen and the dining room had been wide open. The woman could have heard every word Julian and she had said.

"What's the matter?" asked Julian.

Meg lowered her voice. "I think Mrs. Prentice heard us talking. I saw her leave the dining room."

"So?"

"Well, maybe it's O.K. But last night, after I was talking with you, I heard a click on the line like someone hanging up the phone. She was the only one who could've been listening. And she didn't look surprised when Mr. Young told her about Kathy."

"Oh, the nosy type." Julian didn't sound worried.

"Well — let's go then." Meg kept thinking about Mrs. Prentice as she whisked Julian's dishes from the table and stacked them in the dishwasher with hers. Then she led the way out the front door.

Meg paused at the top of the terrace steps, studying the scene before her. The lawn, which stretched to the road, was shaded by two big-crowned live oak trees. Wide beds of petunias and geraniums bordered the loop of the driveway. Beyond the road was more grass as far as the stone wall, and from there a strip of sandy beach sloped gently to the bay.

For once, Heron was not on the seawall or the long pier. The only person Meg could see was Pedro, halfway between the house and road, weeding a flower bed. Nearby, a pair of ground doves walked daintily, making their sad, cooing sound.

Meg ran down the steps and caught up with Julian, who was already opening the car door for her.

"Let's go over and talk with Pedro," suggested Meg. "Maybe he saw the van. He's in the front yard a lot of the time."

Pedro knew about Kathy's disappearance. "I hear it on radio," he told them. But when asked, he denied seeing the van. "Radio say Kathy picked up after dinner. I go in house five-thirty. Not go out again."

Meg knew that the gardener lived in a neat little cottage behind the Youngs' house, and it was true he couldn't see the road from there. So they could cross him off as a witness or a suspect — if he was telling the truth.

As they drove along, Meg wondered, How could you tell when someone was being truthful?

They had gone only a short distance when Julian nosed into the parking area in front of a tiny building called the Oyster Shack. People came here to buy fresh oysters, right off the boats. Behind the building was a dock, and in front of it a public phone booth.

"I'm going to call in my news," he said. "Don't go away." He fished in his shirt pocket for a small notebook.

Why hadn't he called at the house? thought Meg, and then at once realized it was probably because of Mrs. Prentice.

She wanted to warn him, "Be careful what you say!" But she kept still. Julian knew as well as she did what was safe to put on the air.

Just then she noticed someone coming down the road. The tall, slow-moving figure topped by the cap with the pointed visor was all too easy to recognize. Even now, when she had been assured he was only an innocent summer visitor, she couldn't bear to see those staring blue eyes.

To her relief, Heron was still some distance up the road when Julian returned to the car.

He got in behind the wheel. "Isn't that the fellow you and Kathy were so upset about?"

"Yes. I found out his real name's Sidney Tripp," said Meg. "Mrs. La Rose told the sheriff he's O.K., but I still don't believe it."

"Let's talk to him, then." Julian opened the door.

Meg drew back. "I don't want to. Anyway, Mrs. La Rose said he was playing bridge with her last evening so he couldn't have seen the van go by."

Julian put his hand on her cheek and gently turned her face toward him so she had to meet his eyes. "You're afraid of him, aren't you?"

Meg shrugged. "Well —"

"I can't believe it. I never knew you to be scared of anything or anybody."

It was a challenge. "I guess we ought to talk to him." She climbed out.

"Good for you!" Julian spoke under his breath, for Mr. Tripp was now within a few feet of them.

"Hi!" Julian called out pleasantly. "We'd like to ask you a question."

The man paused. "Well?"

Meg was standing next to Julian. Seen up close, the blue eyes were cold and yet piercing. His thin face, with the pointed nose and small mouth and chin, was more birdlike than at a distance. It took courage for Meg to stay there.

Julian asked, "Did you happen to notice a brown van around here the past day or two? One with brown-and-yellow striped curtains in the windows?"

"What business have you asking questions?" demanded Tripp. "Let's see your police badge."

"I don't have one," Julian admitted calmly. "I'm a friend of Kathy Young's, trying to uncover any evidence I can find."

"Take my advice and leave it to the police," said Tripp. He walked around Julian and continued down the road.

Julian's face turned red, and, when he got into the car, he slammed the door.

Meg sat beside him, seething at the man's rudeness.

Before Julian turned the key in the ignition, he said, "I have to apologize to you. When you and Kathy told me about how this fellow Tripp was watching you, I didn't take you seriously. Now I can see why you were upset. What a character!"

Meg felt a glow of pleasure. Finally someone believed her.

They continued north on the road, traveling slowly so Meg could watch for people they might question.

Suddenly she stiffened. "Julian! Stop!"

He put on his right-turn signal and pulled over. "Are you trying to give me a heart attack?" he asked.

Without answering, Meg pushed the door open and jumped out. She began to run back in the direction from which they had come.

She had glimpsed something lying beside the road. Something that looked like a dog. A big dog. Where was it?

There. Just ahead of her. She slowed to a walk as she approached the dusty heap sprawled on the shoulder of the road.

Yes, it was an animal. The fur was so thick with dust it was impossible to tell what color it had been. But it was a dog and it was the same size as Rusty.

Meg knelt on the ground and bent over the still form, not even noticing that Julian was there until he crouched beside her.

"It's Rusty, isn't it?" he asked.

Meg nodded, unable to speak.

Julian said, "He doesn't look as if he'd been hit by a car. Do you think he's alive?"

"I — I don't know," Meg managed to say. "He hasn't moved."

A New Lead

Julian stood up. "We'll have to take him to the vet — fast. We ought to have something flat to move him on." He looked frantically around. "I know! I'll go back to the Oyster Shack. They'll have a board of some kind."

"Oh, yes, please!"

Julian raced off.

Meg sat down on the gravelly edge of the road. Her left hand rested gently on the dog's side, while with the other hand she stroked his head. His body felt warm, but the sun would heat his fur, so that was no test. Then she noticed something else, a faint up-and-down movement under the palm of her left hand.

She shouted after Julian. "Drop off my purse on your way back!"

He lifted his hand in answer and kept on running toward the car.

In a short time he had turned the car around and was stopping beside her. He handed out the purse without asking any questions, and waited while she burrowed for her compact, opened it, and held the mirror in front of Rusty's nose. She bent low to study the result. Yes, a slight mist clouded the mirror.

"He's alive!" She said it softly at first, then added jubilantly, "He's breathing!"

"Praise be!" said Julian. He slid back under the wheel and sped off down the road.

Meg closed the compact and dropped it into her purse. Then she shifted her position so she sheltered Rusty from the sun.

He must be thirsty, but she had no idea where she could get drinking water nearby. "The vet will give you a drink," she whispered.

But Julian had been thinking of this, too, and when he returned, besides an old piece of plywood, he had a Coke bottle full of water. Meg opened the dog's mouth and Julian dribbled a small amount over his tongue. After a moment's pause, Rusty's mouth moved. At the next try, he was able to swallow some of the water.

Working together, Meg and Julian slid the plywood under the dog's heavy body and then lifted him into the hatchback of the car.

Since it was an emergency, they didn't have to wait to see the veterinarian. "Exhaustion," the doctor said after he had checked Rusty. "He must've run after that van until his legs folded under him. And in the heat, and probably without water, it's a wonder he's alive."

"Will he be all right?" Meg asked anxiously.

"I think so. Right now he's worn out and dehydrated. We'll give him liquids intravenously, and some cortisone the same way to take care of shock and stress. We'll get him eating to build up his strength. Call us in a couple of days."

"Thank you," said Meg. She looked back at Rusty on the examining table where the doctor's assistant was already beginning to care for him. She hated to leave.

The doctor walked them to the door. "He's young," he reassured them. "And he's a good, healthy dog. That's in his favor."

When they left the office, Meg was surprised to discover that it was not yet twelve o'clock.

"We got an early start," Julian reminded her. "If you're up to it, we can still talk to Mrs. La Rose before lunch."

The Starfish Cabins were about a quarter of

71

a mile from the Young house, on the corner of Shore Road and a lane that led west to the main highway.

The four little cabins and Mrs. La Rose's house were in a live oak grove. The house and one cabin had a view of the bay, but the other buildings were hidden in the trees.

Julian pulled into the driveway and stopped near the OFFICE sign on the front door of the house.

"Mrs. La Rose has been running this place alone since her husband died about two years ago," he said. "I know her because she always buys shrimp from us. She's been trying to find a manager for the cabins so she can get a job someplace else. The cabins alone don't bring in enough money."

Mrs. La Rose, a slim, attractive woman with blond hair styled close to her head, was willing to tell them about Mr. Tripp. This was his first visit to Oak Point. A lonely man, she said. His wife had died only a few months ago.

"For a few days he went out with Mrs. Ann Morgan. She's in Cabin 4. Then he began to see Essie Prentice. You know her mother, Meg. She keeps house for the Youngs."

Meg nodded silently. She certainly did know Mrs. Prentice.

Mrs. La Rose went on. "Poor Ann," she said sympathetically. "I think she was hurt when

Mr. Tripp dropped her. I know her fairly well. She stayed here last year in November. So I did what I could — asked her and Sidney Tripp in for bridge last night, but he didn't even walk her back to her cabin."

Meg wondered why anyone would want to go anywhere with Mr. Tripp.

"By the way, Julian," said Mrs. La Rose, "I've found just the woman to manage this place. I'm expecting her today."

"Hey, great! Hope it works out for you." Julian turned toward the door. "Thanks for your help."

Meg wasn't ready to leave. "I heard Miss Morgan is a private detective. I'd like to talk to her."

"I'm sure she wouldn't mind if you called on her," Mrs. La Rose assured Meg. "She's in her cabin. I saw her go that way a few minutes ago."

Walking down the path through the trees to Cabin 4, Julian remarked, "If she's a private detective, she may want to be paid for answering questions."

"Do you think so?" asked Meg, worried.

"I'm kidding. Well, sort of. You know lawyers don't like to answer legal questions at parties, and doctors don't want to prescribe for your grandmother's arthritis at a ball game."

"I guess you're right," said Meg. "But I still want to give it a try."

Julian chuckled. "I said you weren't afraid of anybody. O.K. Let's go."

Ann Morgan opened the door to Meg and Julian. She was dressed in light blue slacks and shirt and had some knitting in her hand. Her short brown hair curled softly around her face. She didn't look at all like a toad.

In fact, thought Meg, she was rather pretty when seen up close.

There were two comfortable chairs in the cabin and Miss Morgan gave them to her guests while she perched on the desk chair.

Julian and Meg explained briefly that they were friends of the girl who had been kidnapped.

"Yes, I know about the case," said Miss Morgan, starting to knit on a yellow sweater that appeared to be for a small child. "I've been following the accounts on the radio and TV."

"We know you're a private detective," Meg began. Coming here had been her idea, so it was up to her to talk. "We wondered if you had noticed anyone who might be a suspect or if you had any ideas how we could help."

"The police are working on it, I gather by the news broadcasts." The knitting needles didn't stop. "I doubt if they need our assistance."

Meg squirmed. Julian had been right when he said a professional detective wouldn't give advice to a couple of strangers.

He came to Meg's rescue. "Sheriff Weaver knows what we're doing. He seems to appreciate all the help he can get."

Meg admired her friend's quiet, matter-of-fact manner. That's what comes of being a few years older, she thought, wishing she could match his poise.

Miss Morgan stopped knitting and looked directly at Julian. "Tell me some more about this. What has the sheriff's department done so far?"

"They've found the van," he said, "and it's been identified as the one that picked up Kathy."

Miss Morgan nodded. "Go on." She was knitting again.

Meg added, "They've sent out a bulletin to all police units."

"Naturally," said Miss Morgan. "I trust they also sent out a photo of the girl."

"Yes. Dan Young — Kathy's father — gave one to the sheriff."

The woman glanced at her watch. "It's almost eleven-thirty. There may be a news bulletin on the half hour." She switched on the television.

Soon the special bulletin came on and with it was Kathy's picture.

"Kathy Young, only daughter of wealthy industrial leader Daniel E. Young, was kidnapped not far from her home on Shore Road, north of Oak Point, between eight and eight-thirty last evening." The bulletin continued, "A ransom call has been received by Young."

Meg stared at the screen in amazement.

Julian exclaimed, "Who leaked that? I didn't."

Ann Morgan said sharply, "Listen!" She had dropped her knitting in her lap and was all attention.

But the rest of the bulletin only described the van and said it had been identified.

Miss Morgan snapped off the T.V. "Well, that's a mess!" She looked indignant. "How does the sheriff think the ransom can be delivered now? Someone's sure to try to follow the girl's father to the pickup site."

"Sheriff Weaver sure didn't give out that information," said Julian. "He warned me not to tell about the ransom. And I didn't."

Miss Morgan said sharply, "Someone didn't have your high ethics." The detective stood in the middle of the floor with the knitting at her feet. The yellow ball of yarn rolled across the carpet and Meg sprang to pick it up. The woman accepted it with an automatic "Thank you." She scooped up the half-finished sweater and dropped the whole bundle onto the dresser. "This means your friend Kathy is in more danger than ever. Let's figure out what we can do."

In spite of her gloom over the broadcast, Meg's spirits lifted. "*Will* you help us?" she asked.

The woman answered briskly, "It looks as if I could be useful. First you'd better tell your friend the sheriff to plug that information leak."

"I bet he's upset about it," put in Julian. "He's good at his job."

Miss Morgan relaxed slightly. "He has my sympathy. It's not every day you have a major crime in Oak Point."

"That's right. There's practically no crime," said Julian.

Miss Morgan again sat down, this time without her knitting. "I got that impression as soon as I came. I feel so safe here I never even lock my car doors." She looked from Julian to Meg. "You want to get your friend back home as soon as possible. Is that it?"

"Yes," said Meg.

Julian nodded. "Right."

"If we could locate the girl, that would be the quickest way." Miss Morgan walked over to the window and then turned around. "I have an idea of a likely place to look for her."

Meg and Julian waited eagerly.

"In that old house —"

"The Ogden house!" Meg interrupted. "That's what I thought, too." She was pleased that she and the detective had had the same idea. "I told the sheriff and he's probably there right now."

Julian checked his watch. "He's had time to search the place. He said I should call him in a couple of hours. I want to tell him about Rusty, anyway."

"Rusty?" inquired the detective.

Miss Morgan listened, her bright eyes never leaving his face, while Julian explained. "Use my phone," she said when he had finished.

Meg crossed her fingers. If only Weaver had found Kathy! Rusty had returned; perhaps soon Kathy would be home. She and the woman waited in silence.

After Julian had told Weaver about the dog, his end of the conversation was choppy and not encouraging. "You didn't? . . . That's too bad. . . . No, we haven't. We're with Miss Morgan . . . the private detective. . . . Yes. . . .

That's interesting. . . . Right now? . . . Will do."

Miss Morgan said, "Apparently they didn't find her. Well, it was just an idea."

Julian hung up. "No luck. Weaver says the Ogden place is empty except for a young fellow named Gabe who had been hired to clean up the house. The sheriff says we can come over to his office now if we want to."

His eyes questioned Miss Morgan before he continued. "He has a new lead. One of the shrimpers — a friend of mine — called in. Somebody he knows saw a black-haired kid on a shrimp boat. He didn't get a good look, but he thinks it could've been a girl."

A Special Talent

Kathy slowly climbed back over the rail. The two men who faced her on the narrow strip of deck were crowded against the side of the pilothouse. The moonlight singled out the barrel of the pistol held by the taller man.

The back of Kathy's neck still tingled from the pressure of the muzzle of that gun, but seeing it pointed at her now seemed unreal. There stood two grown men, holding a gun on her as if she were a wild animal.

"Put it down!" Her words were a command. Then, still with dignity, she promised, "I won't jump off the boat."

The man's lips moved and he jerked the pistol in the direction of the main deck.

Kathy couldn't hear what he said but it was plain enough where he wanted her to go.

Once they were on the wide deck, she was led into the pilothouse and the smaller, younger man approached her with a length of rope.

She backed away. "Don't tie me up. I'll stay here."

Again the man with the pistol seemed to be talking. The girl stared at him, feeling helpless and numb with fear. The moon didn't give enough light to read his lips and she had no idea what he was saying. If only Meg were here to interpret for her.

Suddenly the man seized her wrist and flung her onto the pile of nets. Every bone in her body was jarred. She had never before been handled roughly and it made her so angry she lost her fear.

"I can't hear you!" she shouted. "Don't you know I'm deaf? What did you do with my hearing aid?"

The two men stood motionless, staring at her. Then the younger man crouched beside her. She could feel his breath against her face and ear. He must be shouting, but only a faint sound reached her. His breath was strong with tobacco.

She pulled away. "If you're shouting, you

might as well give up. I can't hear without my hearing aid."

The man got to his feet and walked to the door with his companion. They seemed to be talking with each other.

A moment later the young man turned back. In the moonlight that came through the open doorway she could see him making motions. He pointed to the pile of nets on which she lay, and then to her. He put his hands together and rested his face against them.

"You want me to stay here and go to sleep?" asked Kathy.

The man nodded.

"All right," Kathy agreed. "But first I need a bathroom."

The man crossed the pilothouse and lifted the lid on a box that was built in against the wall.

So that was the toilet, Kathy realized. Or, as Julian had told them it was called on a boat, the head.

"And I'm thirsty," she added.

He opened an ice chest such as she and her father used when they went on picnics and fished out a cold can of soda water, dripping with moisture.

"Thank you," said Kathy. "One more thing. May I have a blanket?"

Another box along the edge of the wall produced a coarse blanket.

The men disappeared onto the deck and a few minutes later, feeling more comfortable, Kathy rolled up in the blanket and lay down on the nets. It wasn't a bad bed.

She had lost much of her fear. These men didn't act as if they wanted to hurt her. The one who had tossed her onto the nets had lost his temper because she hadn't done what he asked, whatever that was. She liked the younger one better, the one who had given her the soda.

Neither of them was the driver of the van that had picked her up. The person in the back seat of the van had worn a hood, so she had no idea how he looked.

How many people were in on this? she wondered.

She thought of her father. He always knew what to do, so he'd find her. But how would he know where to start searching? Who'd think that kidnappers would hide a person on a boat?

Tears ran down the sides of her face and into her ears. She felt alone and defenseless. It reminded her of the first few weeks after she had become deaf. Then she had felt cut off from everyone and terribly scared. And angry.

Angry because of her own helplessness and because she couldn't understand anyone. The loss of her mother only a few months before had made everything worse. She was embarrassed now when she recalled how she had cried and thrown things in her rage.

As for her father, he hadn't known what to do, but often he had put his arms around her and held her close. That had told her best of all that he loved her and she wasn't alone, even if she couldn't hear him.

All that was before Dad had found her teacher, her dear Flora. She remembered when Flora had taken her to a place in Brighton to be fitted with the hearing aid.

It had been exciting to hear sounds again, and learning sign language and lip reading had been a challenge, and fun when Meg came to stay with her.

When will I ever see Meg again? she wondered.

Finally, exhausted, she fell asleep.

She was awakened by the vibration of the diesel engine. Where were they taking her?

She opened her eyes to slits and discovered that it was daylight. The taller man was at the wheel only two or three feet from where she lay. He must be the captain of this shrimp boat, and the younger man was the mate.

Soon he turned his head quickly as if someone had called him. Then he hurried onto the deck. Kathy waited several minutes but neither man came back. It must be the captain had put the wheel on automatic pilot.

When no one returned to the pilothouse, Kathy got up and looked out the windows. The boat was in a bay, but the shore was so distant, she knew she couldn't swim to it. No other craft were nearby. It was useless to think of escape now.

With nothing else to do, she stood at the window facing the deck and watched the two men preparing to put the huge cone-shaped net overboard. They worked quickly with no wasted motion. She had seen Julian and his father lower their shrimp net, and these two seemed even more experienced. So they were real shrimpers. Kidnapping must be a sideline to make extra money.

Now they were getting the doors ready. Several years ago when she had first noticed the doors used by shrimpers, she had been puzzled. The men had called them doors and that's what they looked like. But she had wondered why they were connected to the open end of the shrimp nets.

Her father had explained, "They're used to keep the net open and hold it on the bottom where the shrimp are."

But she had not fully understood until she had seen Julian and his father put out their net. How careful they had been to set the doors into the water at just the right angle, so the force of the water and the tug of the lines fastened to them would keep them in the proper position.

The sun shimmered on the deck and the men's hair blew in the brisk wind. Kathy longed to be outside.

She edged through the doorway and stood with her back against the pilothouse, but she had been there only a few seconds when the captain saw her and angrily motioned her inside. Kathy ducked back out of sight, but she continued to watch the men at work by peering through the window or around the edge of the doorway. They were talking to each other, and it was frustrating not to be able to hear even a sound.

Suddenly she became alert. The younger man, whom she had decided was the mate, was facing toward her so she could see his mouth. She read the words, "Hey, Harry! Come here!"

So the captain, the one who had the pistol, was Harry. She felt a glow of satisfaction. How lucky that she could read lips. Perhaps she could find out their plans for her. She'd have to be careful though, not to let them realize she knew what they were saying.

She soon found out that it wasn't as easy to read their lips as she had hoped. The men were constantly moving, and only rarely did they face in her direction. Finally she learned that the mate was named Bill. Another time she caught the word *radio*, and once Bill said something about *the girl*.

When the net was out, Bill came into the pilothouse and took the wheel.

"May I have some water?" asked Kathy. "I'd like to wash, and I'm hungry."

Bill gave her a brief smile as he handed her a pail with a small amount of water, a towel, and a hard lump of soap. Then he produced a cheese sandwich and another can of soda from the ice chest. He was friendly, but unfortunately Harry seemed to be the boss.

There was something about Harry that was familiar. His eyes? Suddenly she thought she knew. The hooded person in the van. The eyes that had shone wickedly through the holes in the hood were like Harry's.

Bill went onto the deck, but Kathy washed as best she could without undressing. There was no knowing when he or Harry would come back.

Afterward she stood in the sunshine in the

doorway to eat the sandwich and drink the soda. Her hair, tossed by the wind, stood up in black feathers.

Now that the net was safely out, the men spent more of their time in the pilothouse, taking turns at the wheel, listening to a radio, or talking on the CB.

About two hours after they had dropped the net overboard, they hauled it back in. Now it was heavy with their catch. Kathy watched while Bill untied the tip end of the net, which Julian had called the cod, letting the contents spill onto the deck.

Both men began to sort out the shrimp and toss the fish they didn't want over the rail. Kathy noticed they kept a few flounder and some big crabs which could be sold in the market. They packed the shrimp in chopped ice in boxes.

Kathy wished she could go onto the deck and help, even though it was a messy job that would have left her smelling fishy from head to foot. Anything would be better than being prisoner in this tiny room.

Finally Bill washed off the deck while Harry came in and spoke on the CB.

Kathy lay down on the nets and watched him, hoping to pick up some information. However, most of the time he stood with his back to her so she had no idea what he was saying. Apparently it was important, for afterward he and Bill talked excitedly to each other, waving their hands and casting quick glances at their captive.

Kathy recognized the word ransom. So she had been right about that. She wondered if her father had paid it.

But something else was bothering Harry and Bill. Something about a black-haired boy.

Kathy lay still and kept her eyes open just enough so she could see the men's lips. She tried not to let her face show any emotion. They mustn't guess that she had her own way of eavesdropping.

Gradually she pieced together the information. Harry had received word that someone had reported seeing a black-haired boy on a shrimp boat. The Coast Guard was searching boats, just in case the black-haired person was a girl.

Her hopes rose, but a moment later she was in despair.

All too clearly she read Harry's words, "We'll get rid of her."

A Black-haired Boy

"Get rid of her?" Bill repeated the captain's words, but his eyebrows went up so Kathy knew he was asking a question.

"Over the rail," said Harry. "I'm sick of this job."

Bill shook his head. "No. Too risky."

"We'll say she tried to swim to shore."

Occasionally Kathy missed a word, but she understood enough to follow the conversation. She found it hard to keep her face expressionless while Harry planned her death.

"That won't work," said Bill. "She might make it to shore."

Harry replied, grim-faced, "We can make sure she doesn't."

"Not me." Bill was firm. "I'm no killer."

"O.K. What's your idea?"

"This." Bill strode over to Kathy. He whipped off his stocking cap and pulled it down over her hair, tucking in a few strands.

"What good'll that do when the cops search the boat?" asked the captain.

Bill didn't answer. His eyes were on Kathy's face. "Are you sure she can't hear us?"

"Positive. It came over the radio. Can't hear a thing without her hearing aid."

"Some deaf people can read lips," said Bill. He leaned over Kathy. "There's a spider on your cheek."

Kathy continued to stare at him, stony-faced.

He tried again. "Watch out! There's a mouse!"

Kathy said, "I told you I can't hear. There's no use shouting at me."

Bill stood up. "Maybe some people can read lips, but she can't." He glanced at Harry. "My idea is she stays here with the cap on. If a patrol boat comes near we'll —" He turned his head and his words were lost to Kathy.

The captain shook his head angrily and said something, but he, too, was out of range of Kathy's eyes. She wished she knew what he was saying, for he didn't seem to agree with Bill.

The two men went onto the deck, still arguing.

In a few minutes the captain entered the pilothouse and took over the wheel. The boat began to go faster.

Were they taking her out to sea to dump her where they were sure she couldn't swim to shore? wondered Kathy. In her mind she saw herself being tossed into the water. She swam and floated for a long time before she saw a boat. As it drew near a wicked fin cut the surface of the water. A shark!

She hastily closed the door of her imagination. No use scaring herself to death ahead of time.

At last, overcome by the warmth in the pilot-house and her own weariness, she again fell asleep.

She awakened suddenly to find Bill and Harry bending over her. Bill rolled her over, pulled her hands together behind her back, and tied them. When he again put her on her back, Harry had a handkerchief in his hands, waiting his turn. She guessed that he was preparing to tie it around her mouth.

"Don't!" she begged. "I'll keep still!"

Harry paid no attention to her plea but quickly stuffed something into her mouth, then tied the handkerchief around her head to hold the gag in place.

Although she turned to Bill and begged with her eyes, he refused to look at her as he lifted her up. Harry raised part of the nets on which she had been lying. Bill lowered her onto the portion of net that was still on the deck. Harry had the rest of the bundle in his hands. Kathy saw it coming and struggled to roll out of the way. But the net came down over her like a tidal wave.

The heavy net hit her with such force it took her breath away. It covered her head and she couldn't breathe.

This is it, she thought.

Then the weight on her head lifted slightly. She breathed as deeply as she could through her nose, longing to open her mouth and draw in great gulps of air. She glimpsed two hands. Probably that was Bill, trying to give her a chance. The hands peeled back the net, then placed three or four thicknesses over her face. Air came thinly through it.

The pressure on her chest was terrible. The pain of her arms which were drawn behind her was a sharper agony. Trying to move took breath and she had none to spare. She made an effort to relax and ignore her pain. Somewhere she had heard that was possible, but it wasn't working now.

Why had they done this to her? It must be they had seen the patrol they had talked about. She hoped the boat would be stopped. If the Coast Guard searched thoroughly they might find her even under this pile of nets.

But the engine's vibration never stopped. The boat seemed to be moving ahead at a steady speed. If someone didn't come soon it was going to be too late. Her whole body was getting numb.

"Help me! Someone help me!" she cried silently.

She felt as if she were going far away. Nothing was real anymore.

When the nets were lifted she could feel the air rush into her lungs in a great *whoosh!*

Bill picked her up and carried her to the open door of the pilothouse. He removed the gag and untied her hands. She was limp, but when he rubbed her arms and legs, feeling began to return to them.

Harry was at the wheel again, and the boat was clipping through the water faster than ever.

Kathy looked up at the sky where small white clouds floated overhead. The world was beautiful and she was thankful she hadn't left it.

"May I have some water?" she whispered.

In an hour she was feeling quite strong. Bill brought her some soup and a sandwich.

While she ate hungrily the men talked to each other, but she didn't try to find out what they were saying.

It was a surprise to her when she discovered the boat was approaching land. No dock was in sight. In fact, the area was bare of houses. Bill was inflating a small rubber raft.

When he had finished he came to her. "We're going ashore," he said, speaking slowly and pronouncing each word carefully. So he did realize she could lip read. She understood exactly what he had said, and because she trusted him, she nodded her understanding.

Getting into the bobbing raft was a tricky operation, but Kathy was strong enough to help herself, and Bill guided her. Harry stayed on board the shrimp boat.

At first Kathy could see nothing on shore except a stony beach and scrub trees. But as they drew nearer, a black panel truck labeled Smith and Smith, Plumbers, came into sight. It stopped near the beach and seemed to be waiting for them.

A man climbed down from the driver's seat and came toward them. Suddenly Kathy recognized him. He was the driver of the van that had kidnapped her!

She seized Bill's arm and pulled back. "Do I have to go with him?"

He stopped and faced her. "Yes."

"I'm afraid of him. Don't let him give me a shot."

He took her hand and talked directly to her. "I'll do what I can."

"Are you going with me?"

"No."

"Am I going home?"

He shook his head, and she saw the pity in his eyes.

The other man had reached them. Kathy gave Bill one last look and said, "Thank you."

In the rear of the panel truck was a rolled-up rug. Bill opened it, then folded it so it formed a thick cushion that covered most of the floor.

On the long, rough ride that followed, Kathy was glad of the rug. Finally she stretched out on it and went to sleep.

It was still daylight when they stopped on a lonely road. The rear of the panel truck was opened and a redheaded young man with a beard to match appeared in the doorway. A blue panel truck was backed up to the one in which she had been riding.

Rug and all, Kathy was transferred to the redhead's truck. Only this time, to her dismay, she was rolled inside the rug.

Miss Morgan Plugs a Leak

Meg looked from Julian to Ann Morgan, trying to read their faces in the dim light of the cabin. Were they as excited as she at the information Julian had just gotten from Sheriff Weaver that Kathy might be hidden on a shrimp boat? That was a new place to keep a kidnap victim! At least it would be better for Kathy than in some cellar or dark closet.

Julian paced restlessly. "The sheriff told me the Coast Guard is taking charge of the search. Some job, trying to check all those boats. Like examining a pack of dogs for a single flea."

"This near to Mexico, there must be a lot of black-haired kids," remarked Miss Morgan.

"What about going over to the sheriff's office with us?" asked Julian.

Ann Morgan said doubtfully, "Police officers aren't usually too keen on having the help of private detectives."

Julian explained, "I told the sheriff we were here with you and he said all of us should come over."

Miss Morgan got off the desk chair and walked across to the window, where she turned around and faced them. "Tell you what. You go ahead and talk to the sheriff, find out if he really wants to see me. I have an idea for how we might put the finger on the person who's leaking information to the media, and my plan won't work if I go to the office with you."

"Well, all right," agreed Julian. "What'll we tell Weaver?"

"Ask him to call me as soon as he can from an outside phone. I don't want to take a chance on anyone's listening in on the line," said Miss Morgan. "I'll explain my plan to him then, and if he wants to go along with it, fine. If not, no hard feelings."

Sheriff Weaver was busy, but he quickly agreed to Miss Morgan's suggestion. "Sure, I'll phone your private detective. Come on. Let's all go."

They walked up the street two blocks toward a gas station where there was an outside phone. The hot sun beat down on their heads. Cars went by with all windows closed, using their air-conditioners.

The sheriff wiped his forehead with his handkerchief. "Your friend, Miss Morgan, must find this weather plenty hot. She comes from a town in Wisconsin. We phoned there to check her out, and her story rings true. She's had a small detective agency there for the past ten years. Some law officers don't appreciate outside assistance, but I'll take help anywhere I can get it. This is my first kidnapping case."

Meg and Julian stood outside the phone booth while the sheriff talked to Miss Morgan. When he came out, he was smiling.

A reporter who had trailed them asked, "A break in the case, Sheriff?"

"No, nothing new," Weaver answered pleasantly. "I'll let you know when I have anything."

The reporter wandered off.

On the way back to the office, Weaver explained Miss Morgan's plan to Julian and Meg.

"She's coming over right away, and I'm supposed to keep her waiting. You two come in the office with me. Then I can honestly tell my secretary I'm busy."

"What will Miss Morgan do then?" asked Meg.

"When she's ready, she'll act impatient and ask my secretary again if she can see me."

As it turned out, Ann Morgan waited outside the sheriff's office for fifteen minutes before she told the secretary she was in a great hurry and couldn't stay much longer.

When the sheriff admitted her, the woman's face was beaming.

"I have the answer!" she said quietly. "But first, my credentials." She removed two cards from her wallet and handed them to the sheriff.

So the detective didn't know Weaver had already investigated her background, thought Meg.

Weaver gravely accepted the cards and placed them in the top drawer of his desk.

"Thanks. I'll return these to you later. And now your answer."

Miss Morgan held out her hand. "A piece of paper and a pencil, please."

Meg understood the reason for that request. The room might be bugged. Someone could be listening to every word that was said.

When she had the paper, the woman wrote on it and handed it to the sheriff.

Meg studied Weaver's face as he read the penciled note. At first he looked surprised;

then he nodded and murmured, "Could be." He passed the paper to Meg and Julian.

The only words on it were: The clerk in the next office.

The clerk in the next office. That would be Essie, Mrs. Prentice's mousy daughter, as Julian so aptly called her. Meg met Julian's eyes.

He nodded and said softly, "It fits." Meg knew he was recalling how Mrs. Prentice had listened to their telephone conversation and again had eavesdropped as they talked in the kitchen. Perhaps she was passing information to Essie. But why?

Weaver pushed back his chair. "I'll treat you all to lunch."

It was after two o'clock, and Tom's Waterfront Lunchroom was almost deserted. The sheriff's group had a table by itself, facing the bay. All four ordered hamburgers, and Weaver requested a plate of assorted doughnuts to munch on while they waited.

Meg was amazed that a grown man would have an idea like that. Her mother would be horrified. Dessert first! As for herself, she decided to make the most of the opportunity. Her first choice was a peanut stick.

"How did you zero in on Essie?" the sheriff asked the detective.

"It was easier than I dared hope." Miss

Morgan selected a cream-filled doughnut. "From where I sat, I could watch the switch-board operator and the clerk. Essie, you called her?"

Meg nodded. She wondered if Miss Morgan knew the woman who had taken her place with Mr. Tripp.

The detective went on. "The door to her office was open enough so I could see the phone on her desk. In a building the size of that, it's easy to hear the phone ringing in the various offices. Every time a call came in, no matter who it was for, Essie picked up the receiver. She had a phone with several buttons. She listened all the way to the end of each conversation."

Julian grinned. "If she had her smarts, she'd have closed the door, at least."

"I can see she could pick up a lot of information on the telephone," said Weaver. "But was that her only source?"

"No. I'm sure she gathered interesting items from reports she had to file and possibly from conversation with others who work here. And as to how she delivered her scoops," continued Miss Morgan, "about five minutes before I asked to see you, she left her office to go out-side. I followed at a distance and saw her talk-ing to a reporter in the parking lot, perhaps passing on her latest news nugget."

"Why, that sly boots!" exclaimed Weaver. His broad face shone with admiration. "You're a doggone good detective, Ma'am!"

"Thank you." Miss Morgan nodded modestly.

"Well," said Weaver. "I'll appreciate any help from a person of your background and ability." He paused and frowned. "I don't know how much pay I can round up, though."

Miss Morgan smiled. "I'll take it out in doughnuts. These are delicious."

The sheriff reached across the table. "I'll shake on that."

The woman laughed and held up both hands. "I'm too sticky. That cream doughnut got the best of me."

"Why did Essie give news to the reporters?" puzzled Meg. "Would they pay her?"

Weaver brushed a crumb from his shirt. "Probably not. It's my hunch Essie did it because she's a natural snoop and she likes to feel important. Y'know, I've noticed news leaks several times lately. I'll bet Essie has given out information before."

A group of reporters sat down at the table next to theirs, close enough to hear what they were saying. From then on they said nothing more about Essie, or Kathy's kidnapping.

When they were outside the lunchroom, Weaver said, "I have a difficult task. I'm going to have to tell a certain young lady that we don't seem to have enough work for her." He smiled at the three serious faces before him. "I don't plan to mention the real reason why I'm letting her go, but she may be able to read between the lines."

Alone in the Dark

As soon as Kathy felt the vibration of the rear door of the truck slamming shut, she began to try to fight her way out of the rug into which she had been rolled.

Cleopatra and I, she thought. Somewhere she had heard that Cleopatra had been carried to Caesar rolled in a rug.

At first she hoped she could just unroll the rug, but after several tries she realized it was tied. Then she hoped to wriggle out, but that didn't work, either. Soon she was so hot and out of breath she had to rest. Just as she was again ready to struggle, the truck halted and someone — she assumed it was the redhead —

opened the door and pulled her out, rug and all.

She guessed that it was early evening from the way the light filtered down to her through the open end of the rolled-up carpet.

Although she didn't know where she was, as soon as she was outside the truck she screamed as loudly as she could. As if in answer, the man who was carrying her broke into a trot. In a few seconds they were inside a building. They crossed a room and went up two flights of stairs.

Finally Kathy felt herself being lowered onto the floor, and then she was unrolled dizzily. In the dim light of the single electric bulb in a wall sconce, she saw a high-ceilinged room that once must have been beautiful but now looked as if it had been bombed. Some of the plaster was gone from the walls, leaving the brown lath exposed. Huge shutters covered the windows on the inside. A mattress lying on the bare floor was the only furnishing. Across it was draped a shabby blanket.

At once Kathy knew she was in the old Ogden house. She and Meg had been in it more than once, and she had read a newspaper article about it. The house, more than a hundred years old, had been built solidly to withstand hurricanes, and it had had plumbing long before most homes did.

This place was on Shore Road between her home and Meg's! Surely someone would find her here.

Even if no one came to rescue her, she knew the layout quite well, so she might be able to escape. She judged she was on the third floor in the northeast bedroom, facing the bay.

The redhead went out, locking the door after him. Kathy leaped up and began to examine the room, first checking the shutters. All were fastened and nailed shut. An open door to the right of the fireplace led, as she remembered, to an old-fashioned bathroom where she found soap and a clean towel. When she opened the hot water faucet, she found to her delight that warm water came out. Tonight she'd have a bath and wash her hair in that big porcelain tub with the claw feet.

So far all the evidence made her more sure that this was the northeast bedroom, but there was one thing that would prove it — the secret panel. She went back into the bedroom and crossed to the clothes closet on the far wall.

Inside the closet it was almost completely dark, but Kathy didn't need to see. She ran her hands lightly over the rear wall, searching for the thin edge of the panel. Ever since she had lost her hearing she had discovered that her other senses had become more acute. That included her sense of touch.

There it was, the edge of the panel, just as she had remembered. It should slide sideways, making an entrance into a storage area under the eaves. Best of all, on the far side of the storage room was another panel that opened directly into the south bedroom. Tonight she might be able to use this route to escape.

But something was wrong. Push as hard as she was able, she couldn't move the panel. Again her fingers explored and found the answer. The panel was nailed solidly shut. Without any tools, it would be impossible to loosen those nails.

Afraid that the redhead might find her there, she gave up and returned to the bedroom. When the young man came back she was seated on the mattress, looking as if she had not stirred from the spot.

Her jailer gave her a can of soda and a paper plate containing a hamburger on a roll. He stayed while she devoured it hungrily.

"I wish we could talk, but I can't hear," she said when she had finished eating.

He nodded and pointed to his head.

"You know?" asked Kathy. "You already knew I couldn't hear?"

Again he nodded.

"Do you know where my hearing aid is?"

The man shook his head.

He seemed pleasant enough, but it might be better not to let him know she could read lips. Anyway, with that beard he had, she might not be able to see his lips well enough.

"Paper," she said. "If you bring paper and pencil, you can write what you want to say."

He shook his head and motioned with his hands, palms up.

What did that mean? "You don't have any paper?" she asked.

This time he pantomimed writing and then shook his head.

"You don't know how to write?" guessed Kathy.

He nodded agreement.

Kathy smiled at him. She held up her right hand with thumb and finger measuring about an inch. "A little?" she asked. "Can you write a few words?"

The redhead smiled and shrugged, then got to his feet and left. As before, he locked the door behind him.

Half an hour later he returned, carrying a pencil and a newspaper printed in Spanish.

"Are you Mexican?" she asked. He certainly didn't look Mexican with that red hair.

He nodded and grinned. Then, with the stub of pencil, he printed on the border of the newspaper the word *Si*.

Kathy said, "That means yes." She held out her hand for the pencil and when he gave it to her, she wrote the word *Yes*. "What's your name?" she asked.

Slowly he printed the word *Gabe*.

She read it out loud. "Gabe?"

He nodded and pointed to the *Si*.

"I'm Kathy." She printed her name on the edge of the newspaper.

It was a slow way to talk but gradually she learned that Gabe's mother was Mexican and his father was a German living in Mexico.

The picture emerged of a boy who had often been hungry and had had little schooling.

She looked into the intelligent eyes that peered out beneath the bushy red hair. "Who told you I was deaf?"

He wrote *Bos*, then hesitated.

"Boss?" suggested Kathy.

His head bobbed.

"Who's your boss?"

Gabe shook his head and again pointed to the word he had tried to print.

"Did the boss tell you to watch me?"

"*Si*." Gabe's head went up and down.

His boss must be the head of the kidnappers, reasoned Kathy. So far she doubted that she had seen the boss, unless it was Harry, who she was quite sure was the hooded person in the brown van.

"Does the boss have a beard?" she hazarded.

"No." Gabe shook his head. His answer was the same when she inquired, "Is he fat?" But when she said, "Is he tall?" he nodded emphatically.

"Thin?" she continued.

He pointed to the word *Si*.

Harry was quite tall, but he wasn't thin. However, she knew someone who was both tall and thin.

Kathy jumped to her feet. "Does he look like a big bird?" She did an imitation of Heron, hunching her shoulders and thrusting her head forward.

Gabe laughed and again put his finger on *Si*.

Kathy's excitement increased. Meg had been right. No wonder Heron had followed them around. He was looking for the best time to kidnap her.

Directly in front of her, on the wall beside the fireplace, was a clear patch of plaster. She snatched up the pencil from the floor and drew a hasty sketch of a heron, standing in the reeds.

"This kind of bird," she said.

Gabe studied the picture, then gave her a

quick, sly look out of the corner of his eyes before he nodded. His expression worried Kathy. He looked — sneaky.

"When can I go home?" she asked, hoping to catch him off guard.

He shrugged, then turned and went out of the room.

As soon as Gabe left her alone, Kathy explored her prison more thoroughly. The window shutters were strong and, no matter how hard she pulled, she couldn't open any of them. If only she had something she could use to work on them. On her hands and knees she made a search of the floor. Finally she found a large nail against the wall in the corner near the bathroom.

She had just poked the point of it under one of the shutters when the door opened. Quickly she thrust the nail into the pocket of her jeans.

Gabe came directly toward her and pulled her away from the window. He shook his head and frowned fiercely. He touched the shutter and then slapped his own hand.

Kathy giggled. His message was clear. She was supposed to leave the shutters alone. But as soon as he went out again, she would have another try at opening one of them.

"I wish I had something to read," she said wistfully.

Gabe grinned and reached for the bulb in the wall sconce. Again his face wore a mischievous expression.

"Oh, no!" exclaimed Kathy. "Leave me the light."

For an answer he unscrewed the bulb and went out the door.

Kathy rushed over to the wall fixture and felt around it. Yes, he had taken the bulb. She was alone in the dark.

The Secret Room

Gabe was gone and had taken the electric bulb with him. He — or the boss — was afraid to have a light up here at night for fear a glimmer would show outside. Someone might notice it and wonder who was using the room. By now everyone for miles around must be looking for her.

Well, she'd manage the best she could in the dark.

She felt her way to one of the windows facing the bay and, with the nail, began to pick at one of the slats.

The shutters were old, but she soon discovered that they were not rotten. For over an hour she worked, poking under one slat after another, hoping to find one that was loose.

Her fingers were getting sore so she wrapped one end of the towel around her hand to ease the friction.

All of the slats were solid, she discovered, so she set to work steadily on one that was easy to reach. At last she felt it give way at one end. From then on it was less difficult. After she had removed that strip of wood she set to work on the next.

When she had taken out two, she decided that was enough. She groped around on the floor until she located the Mexican newspaper. The pencil had disappeared, but she could get along without it. Already she and Gabe had written enough on the edges of the front page. In the dark she couldn't tell the front page from the back so, just to be sure, she removed the first and last pages and wadded them into a tight ball which she thrust into her pocket. Then she scattered the other pages so Gabe wouldn't notice at once that some of the paper was missing.

She went back to the window. The next job was to break the glass. Since Gabe might hear the noise of the pane shattering, she must be sure she was ready in case he came back.

The nail. She might need that again. Where

could she hide it? She decided on the mattress. She poked a hole through the ticking and thrust the nail deep into the musty filling.

With the towel again wrapped around her hand, she seized the two slats she had removed, poked them through the gap in the shutter, and rammed them against the window. On the third try she was successful. She couldn't hear the glass breaking, but she could feel the ends of the wood slide through the opening. After that she battered at the broken edges of glass to make the hole larger.

Next, she tossed out the ball of newspaper sending it as far as possible.

That was all she could do, and Gabe might arrive at any moment. She lay on the mattress on her stomach with one hand on the floor, waiting tensely for the tremble of the boards that would tell her he was running up the stairs.

When he burst into the room, she was covered with the old blanket. She hoped she looked as if she were asleep.

The light from Gabe's electric torch beat against her closed eyelids. She opened them sleepily.

"What do you want?" she asked.

I'll bet he wishes he could tell me, she thought with amusement.

She watched him train the flashlight on the windows, one after the other. Suddenly he discovered the broken shutter and dashed over to examine it. He shoved his arm through the opening, then came over to Kathy and shook his fist at her. For a moment she thought he was going to hit her, but instead he walked away and again looked at the window.

While he had his back to her, Kathy got onto her knees on the mattress. Gabe had left the door ajar.

Softly she stood up, then rushed toward the open door. She was halfway down the first flight of stairs when he caught her. He seized her by the shoulders and shook her furiously. Clamping one hand around her right wrist, he dragged her up the steps.

In the room he flung her onto the mattress, then went back and locked the door.

Kathy sat up and rubbed her wrist while she watched Gabe study the broken window as if trying to decide what to do. She hoped someone outside would see the glow of his flashlight.

After a while he crossed to the closet where the secret panel was located. Was he thinking of putting her into the storage room? Kathy shuddered at the possibility of being shut into that windowless space. But it might be a lucky move. Perhaps he didn't know about the opening on the other side.

Suddenly he rushed out of the room. Kathy scrambled to the door to see if it were locked. Yes, this time he had remembered.

Now was her chance to attract the attention of a passerby. She hurried to the broken window and peered through the hole she had made in the shutter.

Tonight the bay was a molten mirror, reflecting a thin, late-rising moon. Staring out through the narrow opening, she felt as if she were gazing down at the world from another planet.

The road beside the shore was deserted. She looked as far as she could to the north and south, hoping to see a movement that would tell her someone was near, but no car or late jogger came by.

What else could she throw out that might give a clue that she was hidden inside?

A sneaker! She hated to part with it, but it was for a good cause. Quickly she slid one off and flung it as far as she could. Since it was heavier than the newspaper ball it would go farther.

She was pulling off her other sneaker to send after the first when she felt the faint movement of the floor that told her Gabe was returning. She darted away from the window just in time and sat down on the mattress with her bare foot tucked out of sight. If he knew her sneaker was on the front lawn, he'd rush out and get it.

Paying no attention to her he went directly to the closet. His flashlight shone against the brown, paneled wall. Kathy sat on the edge of the mattress, watching him pull out the nails. He's saving me a lot of trouble, she thought.

At last he pushed aside the panel, then gathered up his tools and placed them near the door to the hall. When he turned around his light shone full in Kathy's face. He started toward her.

"No! Don't!" she cried. Now that the panel was open and she could see the blackness of the storage room, she was panic-stricken at the thought of being locked in there. What if the door into the south bedroom was fastened shut? She'd be sealed in like a canned sardine.

She jumped up and hid in the corner. Instead of following her, he seized one end of the mattress and pulled it after him. When he came to the door of the storage room, he had to double up the edges to get it through.

Soon he appeared again, and this time his light followed Kathy relentlessly until he caught her. Though she struggled all the way, it did no good. Gabe pushed her into the low-ceilinged room, and moments later she could feel the floor shake as he nailed the door shut.

While he was still hammering, she made her way along the right-hand wall, hunting for the door to the other bedroom.

There it was, quite easy to locate, but it was also easy to feel the sharp points of the nails that had been pounded in to keep it closed.

Kathy crawled across the floor, searching for the mattress. When she found it, she lay down and gave in to hopelessness.

Again she was alone in the dark, only this time was worse than before. Here there was no hope of escape.

And I didn't even get a bath, she thought sadly.

Broken Window

Mr. Young had gone out and Meg was alone, clearing up after breakfast. The evening before Mrs. Prentice had quit with no explanation, except to say she had decided to move to Brighton.

Kathy's father had said he wasn't really hungry, and Meg was still too full of doughnuts to want to eat much. So she fixed some peanut butter and jelly sandwiches, and they ate them on the terrace. Then Mr. Young had carried the housekeeper's suitcases downstairs, and she had ridden away in her friend's vintage car.

When she was gone, Mr. Young commented, "She saved me the trouble of firing her." Sheriff Weaver had told him of Essie's eavesdropping. It seemed that the girl had broken down and confessed, without even being asked, that her mother had given her information about the ransom.

The sharp ring of the door broke into Meg's thoughts. She hastily set down the empty cereal dishes she was carrying and ran to the front door. Who could be coming this early?

It could be a reporter. Several had been there the night before and many had phoned. Mr. Young told all of them that he was not delivering the ransom that night.

"I'd appreciate it if you'd give me a break," he'd said. "Sheriff Weaver's office will give you all the news we think it is wise to release."

Most of them had gone along with the request.

Remembering the warnings Mr. Young and the sheriff had given her, before Meg released the lock she drew aside the curtains that covered the glass in the top half of the door.

To her relief she saw Julian, dressed in a blue knit shirt and dungarees. She quickly let him in.

"I thought you'd be working!" she exclaimed.

"I took the morning off and got one of my pals to fill in for me. I had the idea you might need a taxi." Julian followed her to the kitchen. "I was afraid you'd go detecting on your own. I know you. You'd do anything to help a friend." He stacked the few dishes remaining in the breakfast nook. "I'll help so we can make a fast getaway."

"I'm glad you came," said Meg, putting away cereal boxes. "I feel like a prisoner. Everyone says I can't be out alone, and I want to go to the Starfish Cabins and talk some more to Mrs. La Rose. I'd like to know what Sidney Tripp is doing. I still don't trust him. I didn't see him at all yesterday, and, before Kathy was taken away, every place we looked, there he was."

"Has Mr. Young heard any more from the kidnappers?"

"Yes. Last night he got another ransom note. He found it on his car seat. Now that the news leaks have stopped, he hopes he can deliver the money." Meg drew in a deep breath. "Oh, I hope they let Kathy come back soon!"

"Yeah," said Julian sympathetically. "You two are like twins. I can't think of one without the other." He put the milk into the refrigerator. "That's not all good. You both ought to be a little more independent of each other. You're not just half of a pair. You're a person on your own. A swell person."

Meg looked up, surprised at the compliment, and then quickly lowered her gaze to the cups she was adding to the dishwasher rack. "Thanks. I'll talk it over with Kathy — when she comes back."

They decided on bicycles instead of the car.

"Dan told me anytime we wanted to use the bikes, to go ahead," Meg told Julian. "You can use his and I'll take Kathy's."

The air was still morning-cool, and a fresh breeze from the bay sang in the bicycle wheels as they pedaled up the road.

"I called about Rusty this morning," said Meg. "The doctor says he's getting along fine. He's eating O.K. and walking around."

Julian whistled. "Some dog! The way he looked when you found him, I was afraid he wouldn't make it."

To Meg's disappointment, Mrs. La Rose wasn't home, and neither was Ann Morgan.

"Come on," said Julian. "Let's go to Tom's and I'll treat you to a sundae."

Tom's Waterfront Lunchroom, where they had eaten with the sheriff, was on Shore Road past Meg's home, about a mile from the Starfish Cabins.

Meg mounted her bike. "You have great ideas."

Beyond Bayview, Meg pointed out the

black marks on the pavement. "That's where the van took off with Kathy," she told Julian.

The road blurred in front of her eyes as she relived the terrifying moment when she had seen her friend struggling to get away from the kidnapper.

When they came to the Ogden house, the morning sun shone full on the front of the old building.

As always, the place drew Meg's attention. She stopped her bicycle. "Look at it, Julian. The windows have turned to gold."

He halted just ahead of her and gazed up at the house. "All but one." He pointed. "See the righthand one on the third floor?"

It was true. Part of the lower sash of the window didn't reflect the sun.

"It must be broken," said Julian.

"But yesterday there weren't any broken windows. I'd have noticed, because Kathy's father and I walked past here yesterday just after dinner. We went to my house to be sure everything was O.K. there." Meg continued to stare at the window. "We saw the redheaded fellow carry a rug into the Ogden place, and I stopped and looked the house over the way I always do."

"You could miss a broken window if the light wasn't right."

"I suppose so." Meg wheeled her bicycle off the road. "Anyway, I'm going over and get a better look."

The shiny dark green leaves of the live oak trees rustled overhead, and a lizard scooted in front of them as they went up the flagstone walk, now overgrown with grass. Meg stopped beside the birdbath that stood near the front steps.

From this viewpoint there was no mistaking the broken window on the third floor. Irregular points of glass edged the lower sash like transparent shark's teeth.

"Is that a hole in the shutter?" asked Meg.

Julian moved to the right so he was directly in front of the broken window. "I think it is."

Meg followed him, her heartbeat increasing in response to a new idea. "What if that wasn't just a rug that man carried into the house last night?" she whispered.

Julian's eyes shone like black coals. "Right! I believe you're onto a real clue. Let's call the sheriff!"

As Meg ran lightly across the overgrown lawn, her foot kicked something that wasn't a weed. When she picked it up, it turned out to be sheets from a newspaper that were rolled into a ball.

Julian asked, "What's that?"

Meg handed him the paper. He turned it over in his hands. "Spanish. An old Mexican newspaper." He squashed it into a tighter ball. "Litter. I'll take care of it."

He would have trust it into his pocket, but Meg's sharp eyes had caught sight of something that wasn't the usual newsprint.

"Wait!" She took the paper and smoothed it out against her knee. Something had been written on the border. She lifted it up to see better, and read the handwritten words *Si* and *Yes*. The writing of the word *Yes* was familiar.

Julian looked over her shoulder. "Some Mexican was practicing his English lesson."

Meg turned the paper around and squealed with excitement. Two more words leaped out at her from the margin: *Gabe* and *Kathy*.

She held up the paper with shaking hands. "That's the way Kathy writes her name. I'm sure it is!"

Julian glanced back at the house. "She may be there now! Come on! Let's get help!"

A cream-colored, four-door Ford was coming slowly down the road from the north, and it came to a stop in front of the house. Miss Morgan climbed out.

"I was trying to find you," she called to Meg. "When I couldn't get you on the phone, I was afraid you might be out alone."

Meg and Julian hastily explained their discoveries.

Miss Morgan got back into the car. "I'll go after the sheriff and you stay here to see that no one tries to leave."

She was off and down the road in an instant.

Meg returned to her bicycle. "Let's go up the lane to the back of the house," she suggested. "That looks like the only door that's used."

"We ought to watch the front, just in case," said Julian.

"You're right. How about we stand off to the side where we can see the front and back?"

They waited impatiently beside a tall palm tree. All was quiet around the house. Meg noticed that the blue truck was gone.

In fifteen minutes a police car pulled quietly up to the back porch of the Ogden house. Miss Morgan, who was behind it, parked her Ford out of the way on the road.

Meg saw one of the deputies hurry to the front yard and take his post near the porch. With that exit guarded, she and Julian pushed their bikes to the rear for a better view.

Miss Morgan motioned them into her car. "Get in the back. And if there's any shooting, hit the floor."

Sheriff Weaver, pistol in hand, followed by

one of his men, climbed the steps to the back porch. Weaver knocked and waited. When there was no response, he knocked again and called out, "Police! Open up!"

Again there was no answer from inside the house. Weaver took hold of the doorknob and, to Meg's surprise, the handle turned and the door opened.

The three in Miss Morgan's car waited tensely.

"I hope there won't be any shooting," whispered Meg. "Kathy might get hit."

Meg Finds a Heron

The next ten minutes seemed endless to Meg. When Sheriff Weaver finally came out alone, she was so excited she jumped out of the car and ran to meet him. Julian and Miss Morgan followed her.

"Empty," said Weaver. "But I'm sure Kathy was held here. Someone has been using the room with the broken window, and we found a mattress and blanket in that storage room off the closet." The strain of the past two days showed in his face. His brows were drawn together and his eyes had a tired, worried expression. "They can't have been here more than a few hours. We checked this place yesterday morning."

"May we see the room where you think Kathy stayed?" asked Meg.

"Yes. Wait a few minutes. My deputies are getting fingerprints."

Julian said, "Meg, I have to leave now. Dad will be coming in and I want to help him unload and clean up. Give me a raincheck on that sundae?"

Meg nodded. "I won't let you forget."

As soon as the sheriff gave them the go-ahead, Meg and Miss Morgan climbed the dusty stairs to the third floor. They passed large rooms with high ceilings, decorated with plaster wreaths and flowers, some crumbling.

Entering the bedroom with the broken window was like walking on a stage after the play was ended.

Kathy was here! thought Meg. Her chest ached with the longing to see her friend. It was painful to imagine Kathy in this bleak room. Was she the one who pried out the slats and broke the window? Probably. She had a lot of fight.

Miss Morgan was walking around studying the floor. "I believe the mattress was in this room," she told Meg. "And then it was dragged out. See, there's a clean path through the plaster dust to the storage room."

"You sure know how to notice things," said Meg.

Miss Morgan chuckled. "I didn't study Sherlock Holmes and Agatha Christie for nothing."

The white walls had been marked by many visitors. Meg circled the room, reading names and dates scratched or written on the plaster.

Suddenly she came to a halt. To the right of the fireplace she saw a small picture, a pencil sketch that stood out among the hasty scrawls most people had left. She crouched to study the drawing. The light was poor, but she could make out a bird, standing in the water with reeds around its thin legs. The longer she stared, the more details she could see. The neck was telescoped and the wings were folded close to the body, giving it a hunchbacked look.

"Miss Morgan!" she called. "Look at this picture. What do you think it is?"

The woman bent to study the drawing. "Why, that's a little work of art! It's a heron, true to life."

"That's what I thought." Meg controlled her excitement. She had to be sure. She knelt beside the wall and looked again at the sketch. The reeds around the heron's legs seemed to have a design. "See here," she said, "do those reeds look like letters to you? Like K. Y.?"

"K. Y.?" cried Miss Morgan. "Kathy Young!" She studied the drawing and leaped up. She flung her arms around Meg. "It is!

It's proof she was here! We have to show this to your friend the sheriff."

While the woman went out to find the sheriff, Meg ducked through the low entrance to the storage area where the mattress lay. What a gloomy place. Even with the panel open, the room was like night.

When Miss Morgan returned with the sheriff, Meg came out to join them.

"That's a heron, all right," he said. "What do you make of it, Meg?"

"I think it's a message," she answered. "She's telling us Heron is the kidnapper. Or at least that he's involved."

"I don't see how he can be," protested Weaver. He explained to Miss Morgan. "Meg and Kathy noticed a man they called Heron, actually Sidney Tripp. You know him. He seemed to be following them, so Meg was sure he was the kidnapper. What do you think?"

Miss Morgan considered. "I don't actually know much about him, though we did spend some time together. I will say he's an odd person."

"Well," said Weaver, "I'll have him watched. It does seem as if Kathy must've had some reason for drawing the heron."

The woman asked, "Meg, is that Kathy's style of drawing?"

"Oh, yes. And that's the way she signs her pictures, at least lots of them."

Miss Morgan stood up straight and spoke firmly to the sheriff. "Then I would agree that the drawing was made to give a message, one that only Meg would understand. Kathy knows better than we do who the kidnapper is. This picture makes Sidney Tripp a prime suspect."

Weaver wiped his face. "I find it hard to believe. Look around and see if you can find any other messages."

But the single drawing was all they could locate.

That afternoon, Meg, alone in Bayview, had a frantic desire to go out. She longed to return to the Ogden house to search for more clues. If she had a flashlight she could see better, and perhaps she could find another of Kathy's drawings or even a written message from her.

She paced the floor, going from window to window. Mr. Young was out someplace, perhaps still assembling ransom money. Julian was busy helping his father, so she couldn't ask him to come. If she phoned the sheriff he might send a car to pick her up, but every man was needed to look for Kathy and the kidnappers.

Finally she could stand it no longer. She went outside, locking the door behind her, and sped down the road on Kathy's bicycle with a flashlight in the basket on the handlebars. Who would bother her in broad daylight?

When she reached the Ogden house, she took the lane that led to the rear entrance. One of the sheriff's cars was in the drive and a deputy was standing in the back doorway. She was not surprised at this. But she had not expected to see a familiar tall man coming down the steps from the back porch. With him was a thin young woman with mouse-colored hair. Heron — Sidney Tripp — and Essie Prentice!

The sight of them took her breath away, but she continued toward the house as if nothing had happened. When she drew near she spoke to Essie. The woman murmured "Hello" but did not look up.

She's lost her job, thought Meg, and she suspects I know why.

Mr. Tripp's eyes, shaded by his baseball cap, flicked toward Meg as she nodded to him, but he showed no other sign of recognition.

Meg parked her bicycle beside the driveway and climbed the steps to the back door. Now let Essie and her friend wonder why *she* was going into the old house.

The deputy recognized Meg and let her in.

"I just want to look around again," she explained.

She prowled all through the house from the basement, which had originally contained the kitchen, to the tower, up a few steps from the third floor.

A second deputy was wondering through the rooms, but he didn't interfere with Meg's investigation. She wondered if he had allowed Mr. Tripp and Essie as much freedom.

The only place Meg found any more evidence of her friend was in the storage area off the northeast bedroom. While crawling around on the mattress, she located a large nail that she was sure Kathy had hidden.

Pedaling down the lane toward Shore Road, she wondered what Sidney Tripp and Essie had been looking for. Had they found anything?

Tripp and Essie and Mrs. Prentice. She couldn't help suspecting all of them, even if Weaver did say Tripp was innocent.

And what about Mrs. Prentice's friend, the man who took her to movies? He might be involved, too. Could he have been inside the van that picked up Kathy?

The Boss

Kathy's nose prickled.

The air of the storage room was heavy with dust. When she sat up, too restless to lie still, she bumped her head on a slanting beam.

She slid off the mattress and pulled it out where she had more headroom. Each time she reached up to judge the height of the ceiling, cobwebs clung stickily to her hand.

Now what? she asked herself, sitting cross-legged on the mattress. She had gotten into this spot by breaking the shutter and the window. She could only hope it had been worthwhile and that someone would find the Mexican newspaper she had tossed out. Surely that or her sneaker would lead rescuers to her, even in this hole.

It'll be just my luck if Gabe finds those things, she thought.

Unable to give up hope, Kathy crept across the floor, searching for the hidden door through which she had entered. When she found it, she lay on her back and kicked the panel with all her strength. It did not give. Gabe had nailed it well, and this whole house was built solidly. She wished the walls were plasterboard or plywood as in so many new houses.

For the present, she gave up on the door, but she refused to sit still and do nothing.

She was headed back to the mattress to look for the nail she had hidden in it when she felt a vibration. With both hands on the bare floor, she was in a good position to pick up the faint motion of the wood that told her someone was coming. No, more than one person.

Fear struck her like a blow in the stomach. The second person must be the boss, come to settle with her for the breaking of the window.

With rapidly beating heart, Kathy crawled to the south end of the storage room and crouched against the right-hand wall, to be as far as possible from the spot where the people would enter. Her hope was to see them before they saw her.

Where she was, the storage area shared a wall with the south bedroom. Here the ceiling was high, giving her plenty of headroom.

Suddenly a thread of light like a neon filament outlined the panel that led from the closet to the hidden room. Again she felt a quiver. This time it was in the wall against which she was leaning. She guessed that Gabe was pulling the nails that secured the panel.

While she watched, the panel moved, and then the light went out. What were they doing?

Oh, to be able to hear!

The words of Flora, her teacher, came back to her: "Don't moan about what you've lost. Think about the senses you've gained."

Kathy closed her eyes and concentrated. Someone was coming into the room, groping around trying to find her. Another sense came to her aid — the sense of smell. In this weather everyone perspired and each person seemed to have an individual scent. It was Gabe's scent she picked up. Mingled with the odor of sweat was that of cheap beer.

Kathy sat motionless, not wanting to give him a clue to where she was.

She couldn't sense any other person. Perhaps she had been mistaken and Gabe was alone. In that case, perhaps she could outwit him.

Using her keen nose, she moved away from him. He was on the front side of the storage area, the side toward the bay. That was where the mattress had been.

Kathy worked her way along the opposite wall, circling away from Gabe. Soon she could feel the draft from the open panel. She homed in on the current of air like a plane coming in on radar.

She was through the doorway and across the closet in an instant. Scrambling to her feet, she rushed across the bedroom to the open hall door. The house was in complete darkness, but she knew her way so well she didn't have to pause.

Down the stairs she sped, terrified lest Gabe catch up with her. To her left was the dim oblong of a window. If she went straight ahead, she could run out the back door and be free.

She plunged down the last steps and crashed into a body that was like a solid wall.

A scream tore from Kathy's throat, but was cut off by a hand over her mouth. Although she struggled and kicked, in no time a gag was in her mouth and a blindfold covered her eyes. Someone was tying her arms behind her. That was Gabe. She recognized his scent and the touch of his hands.

The person who had stopped her seemed to have gone, leaving her alone with the redhead.

Kathy relaxed slightly. The way Gabe held her arm she knew she couldn't get away, but he wasn't hurting her. That other person, the one who stopped her, had been rough.

The scent of chloroform approached. Who was bringing it? The boss? She felt a cloth brush against her face and held her breath. When she had to inhale, she was surprised to find that although a cloth was over her nose, it didn't have any scent. Yes, it did. It smelled like Gabe.

He picked her up in his arms and carried her outside and down the steps. The chloroform smell went with them, but it wasn't near her face. Gabe lowered her to the ground and held her by one arm while he opened what seemed to be the door of a truck. Lifting her in gently, he quickly closed the door. The smell of chloroform left with him.

Kathy sat upright and felt of the metal floor and walls with her fingertips. She was in a truck again, but this time without the rug.

Sliding back to the door, she pushed herself up until she found the handle. Yes, of course, it didn't move. She tried in vain to locate a way to release the door lock.

No one had gotten into the front of the

truck. What had happened? Why had someone gone to the trouble to get a cloth soaked in chloroform and then not use it?

She recalled the gentle way Gabe had carried her and had put her into the truck. He had been good to her most of the time.

And now, had he disobeyed the orders of the boss he feared? Was he supposed to put her to sleep and instead had given her a chance? She rubbed her head against the wall, trying to remove the blindfold, but she had no success. It was tied firmly, and without the use of her hands she could do nothing. They, too, were fastened tightly.

The truck jiggled. Someone was in the driver's seat. She didn't feel the vibration of a slamming door, but shortly the motor made the floor shimmy. Now they were moving. She was sure only one person had gotten into the front of the truck. Was it Gabe or the boss?

At first Kathy tried to keep track of the direction in which they were going, but after several turns she gave up.

She wasn't headed for home, that was sure. Perhaps she would be taken into the country and released. That was all right. Anything, as long as she was free. She tried not to think of other possibilities.

Now they were on a rough road. Sitting on

the bare metal floor, Kathy felt every bump like a blow. With her arms behind her, she found it difficult to hold herself upright.

The truck began to slow down, and finally came to a complete halt. Judging by the way the body of the truck shifted, the driver was getting out.

Who would open the rear door, Gabe or the other person, the one who might be the boss?

During the ride Kathy's mind had been numb from the quick change of events and the discomfort of the ride. Now suddenly she was alert.

What if she was right, and the chloroform had been intended for her? If Gabe had driven her here, it wouldn't matter. But that other person — the boss — would expect to find her unconscious — or dead.

Kathy barely had time to slide onto the floor of the truck before the door opened and the cool night air flowed over her. At the first touch of the hands that pulled her out she knew it wasn't Gabe. She let herself slump to the ground. At once she was seized around the waist and hoisted like a bag of flour over a wide shoulder.

In an instant they seemed to enter a narrow path through a field. Bushes whipped Kathy's face and arms. One thorny branch caught the blindfold and tore it away from her eyes, but with her head hanging down, she could see nothing but weeds and the back of a pair of legs.

A few seconds later she was dropped onto the ground next to some kind of building. Kathy considered making a break for it, but her captor didn't give her a chance. At once she was dragged through an open doorway and dumped onto the floor.

A toe shot out and gave her a kick in the leg. Still Kathy did not respond. Perhaps if she pretended to be unconscious she would be left unguarded.

She was quite sure she wasn't being released. What had gone wrong? She knew her father would pay the ransom, but she had heard of kidnappings where the ransom was paid and then the person who was kidnapped was killed.

A flashlight came on nearby. Kathy didn't dare to turn her head but she couldn't resist peering out beneath her lashes. Since she was lying on her back with her head slightly to the right, she could see the ceiling and part of one wall of the tiny building where she lay. The place was only a shack, made of rough, unfinished wood. A few shelves were on the walls and here and there were spikes on which clothing or something had once been hung.

144

Unexpectedly her captor moved into her range of vision. It took all of Kathy's control to keep from drawing in a quick breath. She knew who it was. Gabe tricked me! she thought.

The boss — it must be the boss — stood absolutely still above her with the flashlight trained on her face, probably noticing for the first time that the blindfold was gone.

Kathy lay rigid and terrified. Had the boss caught her with her eyes half open?

The kick that next caught her in the side was no mere nudge to find out if she were unconscious. It was a vicious expression of anger.

The kidnapper knew! Kathy braced herself. This would be the end.

She couldn't believe it when the door closed behind her captor. It could mean only one thing. The ransom had not yet been delivered. Kathy was sure she was being kept alive only in case she was needed to write a note to her father. When the ransom was paid, now that she knew the identity of the boss, she would be wiped out.

Two or three minutes later the door again opened to admit Harry, the captain of the shrimp boat. Harry with the mean eyes. Had he been assigned the job of killing her?

He was carrying an electric battery lamp and two blankets.

Kathy sat up and watched him openly. There was no longer any reason for pretending to be unconscious.

The blankets might be to wrap her body in after he had killed her. On the other hand, perhaps he was her guard and each of them would have a blanket to lie on the rest of the night.

Harry tossed down the blankets and set his lamp on a box before he came over to look at her. Kathy stared back at him with unblinking eyes. Much to her surprise, he reached down and patted her on the head.

A moment later he untied the handkerchief that held the gag in place and cut the rope that bound her hands.

A Shadow
for Sidney Tripp

When Meg left the Ogden house she intended to go straight back to Youngs' and phone Miss Morgan about her discovery of the nail and seeing Mr. Tripp and Essie Prentice.

But on an impulse she rode past Bayview and continued toward the Starfish Cabins. It would be better to talk to the detective in person.

Miss Morgan was sitting at the window of her air-conditioned cabin, a cup of coffee and a plate of cookies from the bakery on the low table beside her. Hunched over her knitting, she did, after all, look a bit like a toad, Meg noticed.

In too much of a hurry to wait, even to take a bite of the cookie she was offered, Meg burst out with her story.

"What a detective you'd make!" marveled the woman. "The nail must be the one Kathy used to break the shutter. But Tripp and Essie — I wonder what they were after?"

"They didn't look too happy. Maybe they didn't find anything." Meg bit into a chocolate chip cookie.

Miss Morgan remarked, "Sheriff Weaver said he'd have Tripp followed. Did you see a car or any of the sheriff's men?"

"Oh, yes," said Meg. "There was a car out in back and a deputy at the door and another in the house."

"But were Tripp and Essie followed when they left?"

Meg frowned. "I didn't see anyone leave, but I didn't go looking. The car was still there when I came out."

"I suppose someone could have been up the road," mused the detective. "On the other hand, I haven't seen any strangers around the cabins. I wonder if Weaver forgot about shadowing our tall friend."

"Friend!" Meg laughed.

"Exactly," said Miss Morgan. "I know what he is and so do you. After seeing that picture of a heron Kathy drew, I can't imagine why the sheriff has any doubts." She knitted faster than ever as if venting her anger on the yarn.

"Anyway," she went on, "I'm not waiting for Weaver to make up his mind. I'm going to trap that heron myself. Did you tell the sheriff about seeing him and Essie?"

"No. I came straight here."

"You'd better tell him. Be careful how you say it in case someone's listening in."

"I will, but it ought to be safe now that Essie's not working for the sheriff." Meg added impatiently, "How are you going to catch Mr. Tripp?"

Miss Morgan let the knitting fall into her lap with her square, plump hands folded over it. Her eyes, round and bright, met Meg's. But instead of answering her question, she announced, "Tonight's the night."

"Oh," Meg felt a shiver of excitement run up her back. Kathy's father must be delivering the ransom money tonight. "I hope it goes all right. Then they'll let Kathy come home!"

"They'd better," said the woman grimly.

"But the trap?" insisted Meg.

Miss Morgan grinned. "I'm going to follow Tripp tonight."

"Do you think you can?"

"Of course I can!" Miss Morgan sounded indignant. "In my business I have to follow people all the time!"

"Oh, that's exciting! How'd you find out about the ransom?"

"The sheriff phoned not more than ten minutes before you came. Didn't Mr. Young tell you?"

"No. I guess he doesn't want to worry me any more than he has to."

"I don't know where it's to be dropped." Again the chubby fingers made the knitting needles fly. "Not even the sheriff knows. But," she added grimly, "I'm sure Tripp knows, and he'll show me the way."

Meg's imagination pictured the two cars flying through the dark, the one in the rear with headlights off.

"But after he picks up the ransom, then what'll you do?" she asked.

"I'll keep on following him. I'm almost certain he'll go straight to the place he's hidden Kathy. Either he'll set her free or —"

"Or what?" Meg felt a cold hand clamp around her heart.

Miss Morgan said reassuringly, "That's why I'm going tonight. To make sure nothing happens to Kathy. You know as well as I do that kidnappers don't always play fair."

On the road back to the Youngs', Meg thought about what Miss Morgan was going to do. It was awfully kind of her to want to make sure Kathy was released unharmed. In fact, it was a great idea. Meg wished she could go, too. Oh, to be there when Kathy was set free!

She could see some problems in Miss Morgan's plan. What if she did follow Tripp all the way to wherever Kathy was hidden. She couldn't arrest him, not all by herself. Maybe she had a weapon, but no doubt the kidnapper had one, too.

Mr. Young was asleep on the sofa when Meg returned to the house.

She tiptoed to the phone in the hall outside her door and phoned the sheriff. When Weaver answered, she said, "I saw Big Bird and Big Mouth today."

"Oh, where?" Weaver sounded amused.

"Coming out of the Den-og ace-play." She hoped the sheriff knew enough pig Latin to figure out she was talking about the Ogden place.

Weaver laughed outright. "You can skip the code talk. All the leaks are plugged in this office, thanks to Miss Morgan. And you don't have to worry about Tripp and his nosy pal. We have a good man watching them. He reported to me about their visit to the Ogden house. They were just snooping around, as usual."

"There's something else I think I ought to tell you."

"O.K. Shoot."

"It's about Miss Morgan. I'm afraid she's going to get hurt."

"How's that?"

"She's going to follow Mr. Tripp tonight."

"What for?"

"She says he'll head for Kathy as soon as he picks up the money."

Weaver moaned. "Oh, good night! I don't think she can get in any trouble following Tripp, but I'll put a tail on her, just the same." He gave a deep sigh. "I'm glad the Texas Rangers are helping us. If they weren't, I wouldn't have enough men. By the way, don't mention the ransom to anyone. We can't take any chances this time."

To Meg's relief he didn't ask if she'd been out alone, and Miss Morgan hadn't seemed concerned, either.

That night Mr. Young bought some fish and French fries for dinner, and he also went to the bakery for rolls and a chocolate cake. Meg made a salad.

In spite of the good food, she could eat only a small amount. Kathy's father scarcely touched his fish. He looked up appreciatively when Meg served the cake and poured coffee. "I'm sure glad you're here." He cut off a bite of cake, then listlessly put down his fork. "I'll have to find another housekeeper. I don't know where to start asking."

"I know someone who's looking for a job," said Meg. "Mrs. La Rose."

Dan glanced up with a trace of hope in his dark eyes. "Kathy'd like her. I wonder if she'd consider coming?"

When Meg had taken care of the few dishes, she found a book and sat down in the living room.

Mr. Young had the newspaper in his hands, but he rarely turned a page. No wonder. He must be planning how he'd deliver the ransom.

Meg, too, found it hard to concentrate on reading. An idea had come into her mind. A plan that was so reckless, so daring, she wondered if it would work.

She gave up trying to read and went to her room. There she took out Kathy's hearing aid that she had found in the van. She put back the battery which she had removed.

The phone in the hall shrilled once and then stopped. A moment later Mr. Young called up the stairs, "Meg, it's for you. Keep it short, will you? I'm expecting a call."

"Right!" she answered. And stuffing the hearing aid into the pocket of her jeans, she ran to the phone.

"Hi, pal!" It was Julian's jaunty voice. Usually Meg loved to talk with him, but tonight she was glad she had been given a reason for keeping it brief. She had too much on her mind and several things she had to do.

She couldn't mention the delivery of the ransom and she certainly couldn't talk to him about her own wild plan.

"Mr. Young asked me not to hold the phone," she said. Then, afraid that he might decide to come over to talk, she added, "I'm really beat tonight."

When she hung up, she thought, That wasn't a lie. She *was* tired. Of course he might assume she was going to bed, but she wasn't going to do that, not for a long time. She wanted terribly to be on hand when Kathy was set free. Besides, she had the battery pack, and her friend would want that.

What she was going to do was dangerous, Meg knew, but if Miss Morgan could risk her life for a girl she didn't even know, then surely she, Kathy's best friend, could take a chance, too.

The Stowaway

Meg went back into the bedroom and closed the door. The attractive room had never seemed more appealing. The bookshelves, the deep chair with the reading lamp beside it, the stereo, and the little color TV all urged her to stay. The feeling of safety here was such a contrast to what she had in mind, she wondered if she should give up her plan.

She had done what she could to help by phoning the sheriff. He would have someone follow Miss Morgan, and his men would be there when Tripp and the detective reached Kathy. Or would they? Sheriff Weaver didn't seem to believe that Tripp was the kidnapper. Perhaps he would send just one man and that wouldn't be enough. Tripp might not be alone. There had been at least two people in the van that picked Kathy up.

No, I have to go, decided Meg. Deep inside she knew that nothing could keep her from going. The love of adventure and the desire to help her friend were part of her very bones.

Dark clothes. They were important. The blue jeans she was wearing were the darkest she had, but her yellow blouse would glow like a candle in the night. She pulled a navy knit shirt from the chest of drawers and changed quickly, afraid at any moment she'd hear the ringing of the phone that might be the signal for the delivery of the ransom.

The timing must be right, or her plan wouldn't work. She couldn't leave here until Kathy's father was gone; yet she had to get to the Starfish Cabins before Tripp set out. That was going to be hard to do. Maybe impossible.

She wished she could leave now, give herself more time. But Mr. Young was too alert. If she tried to sneak out the back door, he'd be sure to hear her. The only thing she could do was be ready to dash out the minute he left.

What else did she have to do? She took her doorkey from her purse and slid that into the pocket with the hearing aid.

Sneakers. The ones she had on were white, but she had a navy pair in the closet.

Finally she rolled her dark-blue hooded nylon jacket into a ball and then sat down to wait, covered by her long robe, full skirted and striped like a caftan. She wore that in case Kathy's father came up to talk to her.

Nine o'clock. When *did* people deliver ransom? No doubt in the middle of the night. She could have a long wait.

There might not be a telephone call! It suddenly occurred to her that she was waiting to hear the phone ring when it might be the other way around. Mr. Young might be going to place the ransom call.

Meg jumped up and ran across the room to open the door. Now she'd have a better chance of hearing the rumble of his voice if he talked on the phone, or the closing of the door as he left. She wouldn't turn on the TV.

Again she waited, trying to read. Even though she was excited, she began to get sleepy. She hadn't had a good night's sleep since Kathy disappeared. Her eyes strayed to the clock. It was nine-thirty. Her head nodded and the book fell from her hands.

She awakened with a start when she heard footsteps climbing the stairs.

"Hi, Meg!" Mr. Young called. "I see your light's still on." He appeared in her doorway, so tall and broad shouldered he seemed to fill the opening.

He was dressed in jeans and an old knit shirt he wore when he worked in the garden.

"I'm going out after a while," he said. "I won't be gone long. For one thing, I'm going to pick up Rusty. He's his own frisky self again. I talked with the doctor a few minutes ago."

So he was taking Rusty along for company when he delivered the ransom. A good idea, thought Meg.

She stretched. "I went to sleep."

Mr. Young smiled at her. "I should think you would. It's after eleven and you usually go to bed early." He lingered in the doorway. "Sorry to leave you alone. I'll lock all the doors."

"I'll be all right," Meg said. "Good night."

"Good night." He still didn't leave. "Thanks for your tip about Mrs. La Rose. She's going to help us out, beginning tomorrow morning."

As soon as he went downstairs, Meg stripped off the robe and pulled on the navy jacket. She stood poised, waiting for the opening of a door, the sound of a motor starting. There was nothing.

She was at the window, waiting for the car to go down the driveway, when the phone rang. Kathy's father must have been sitting beside it because the ring was cut off short.

Seconds later she heard the opening of the side door that led directly into the garage.

Meg turned off her light, shut the door, and sped down the stairs. She waited on the bottom step until the car rolled down the driveway and turned right onto Shore Road. Then she ran to the side door. Since it had a night latch that opened from the inside, she had no trouble getting out and into the garage.

Kathy's bike was where she had left it, standing against the left wall, and Mr. Young had left the garage door open.

It was a strange feeling to be out on a bicycle so late at night. The house lights shone onto the terrace, but the lawn below was dark. The bay, too, was black, except for yellow dots far out that were boats, and the wharf lights that seemed to float in the air. The waning moon had not yet risen.

At the end of the driveway Meg turned left and flew up the road.

Now she felt completely alone. Although it was a warm night, she shivered. It was excitement, she knew, and she drew several deep breaths. That helped.

A car came down the road toward her, traveling fast. She stared hard at it, fearing it might be Tripp, starting out to collect the ransom, but it was a sports car, and in the light from the dashboard she could see a bushy head of hair.

When she neared the cabins, she noticed a car parked beside the road with a man slouched down behind the wheel. That could be the deputy Sheriff Weaver had assigned to follow Miss Morgan to make sure she didn't get hurt.

At the lane that bordered the southern edge of the Starfish property, she turned left. She was going to approach the parking lot from the side and hope no one saw her.

The lights from the office shone through the limbs of the live oak trees. A cabin light winked as she passed.

Meg dismounted and wheeled her bike into the cover of the trees. A palmetto brushed against her leg and she shuddered, afraid she might step on a snake curled up for the night.

She zipped up her jacket and covered her head with the hood. Then, leaving the bicycle, she crept to the edge of the parking lot behind the cottages, staying in the shadow of the trees. She didn't see Tripp's car. Perhaps he had it parked beside his cabin.

To her relief she saw that Miss Morgan's cream-colored Ford had not left. It was in the lot, straight ahead of her.

If Mr. Young's call had been from the kidnapper, telling him it was time to drop the ransom, Meg knew she had no time to spare.

She glanced toward Miss Morgan's cabin a short distance to the right, sheltered by a large tree. A glow shone through the window on the side facing her, but the drapes were closed. The door to the cabin was shut, and she could see no one walking between the cabin and the parking lot.

In fact, no one seemed to be outside.

Meg crept across the grass, slippery with live oak leaves that rustled under her feet no matter how carefully she walked. When she reached the parking lot, she ran to the far side of the detective's car where she would be more hidden.

Miss Morgan had said there was no need to lock car doors around here. Did she mean it? Meg's whole plan would be ruined if the car were locked.

The door opened easily. But to her dismay, as soon as the door was ajar, the ceiling light came on. She hastily crawled onto the floor behind the front seat, pulling the door shut behind her as quietly as possible.

In the dim glow of a lamp beside the walk that led out of the parking lot, Meg made a quick survey of the inside of a car. A sweater and a small pillow lay on the back seat. Nothing was on the floor except for two candy wrappers, which Meg stuffed under the front seat to make sure she wouldn't rattle them.

She decided to lie on the floor behind the passenger's seat, thinking she might be less noticeable there. If it weren't for the hump she could have made herself comfortable. Although she was slim and not very tall, she didn't fit on one side of it.

Fortunately, Miss Morgan's legs were short, so the seat was pulled forward.

After several trials Meg lay on her side facing the back seat and tried to fit herself around the hump.

She was about to turn over again when footsteps approached the car. Meg flattened out as much as possible with her face covered by her left arm.

The footsteps — Miss Morgan's heavy tread — traveled briskly to the rear of the car. A key rasped in the lock and the lid raised. With a crash something landed in the trunk, making the car shake.

The door opened on the driver's side and at once the woman got in and slid the key into the ignition switch. The motor started at the first turn of the key, the car backed up, and turned onto the graveled drive that led to Shore Road.

They were on their way! Meg shivered, but this time with pleasure. She had done it, at least so far.

The floor of the car was an uncomfortable place to ride. She was in no danger of falling asleep.

She wondered where Tripp was. She had thought she would hear his car when it left.

Miss Morgan turned right at Shore Road and right again at the corner, tearing along at a great rate. She must be trying to catch up with Tripp.

At the intersection with the main highway she turned left and traveled south through the village of Oak Point. Here traffic was fairly heavy, even though it was past midnight.

Headlights and street lights made the inside of the car too bright. What if Miss Morgan turned around? Meg knew if she were discovered she'd be put out of the car. The detective would think it was too risky for her to go on this trip.

In a few minutes they had left traffic and lights behind.

Meg had expected to go into the country; she didn't think the delivery of the ransom would be made on a busy street corner. She wished she dared look ahead to see the taillights of Tripp's car. Miss Morgan was driving along in a confident way as if she were sure of where she was going.

The car turned right, then left, then right again, all within a short space of time. It must be difficult to follow a car through this maze.

They were no longer on a paved highway and Meg bounced like a rowboat on a rough sea. She braced herself as best she could, while reminding herself that she had asked for it.

Just as she decided that she couldn't stand another bump, the car stopped with a jolt. Miss Morgan got out quickly. Meg could hear her running across the road and back again. Then the door opened on the passenger's side to allow the woman to slide something onto the floor in front. Something that must be heavy, judging by the way it scraped on the floor.

The door slammed shut and footsteps thudded around to the driver's side. The woman scrambled in and drove off at the same breakneck speed.

Now what was that all about? wondered Meg. She hadn't expected Miss Morgan to pick up anything.

Stalemate

For about ten minutes they traveled at high speed. Then again they stopped. This time Meg heard a click as if Miss Morgan were opening something, perhaps a suitcase. Next there came a rustling sound.

Another click. A fastening was snapped shut.

The car roared off again. Although Meg was jolted worse than before, she paid no attention to her discomfort. She had other worries more serious than a few bruises.

This journey wasn't turning out as she had expected. She was beginning to doubt that Miss Morgan was following Tripp or anyone else.

Some detective I am! she scolded herself. She cowered closer to the floor in silent misery. Now, more than ever, she dreaded being discovered.

At last the car slowed to a stop. Meg knew they must still be in the country for she saw no lights, and when the motor was turned off they seemed to be in a pool of silence.

Miss Morgan pushed down the buttons to lock the doors, then got out of the car. Meg heard her shoes crunch on the gravel beside the road.

When the sound of footsteps became fainter, Meg peered over the front seat just in time to see a dim figure cut across the shallow roadside ditch and enter a field full of weeds and scrubby bushes.

She knew she had no time to waste, but first she had to be sure her hunch was right. Climbing into the front seat, it took only an instant to locate the object Miss Morgan had slid onto the floor and to confirm that it was a suitcase. Seconds later she discovered that it contained the ransom, as she had expected.

It was surprising Miss Morgan hadn't at least put it into the trunk. She must have been in a big hurry. But she *had* locked the car doors this time.

What should I do? wondered Meg. The

smart thing would be to go for help, but she was afraid she didn't have time for that. And where would she look for help out here?

She snapped the case shut and quickly let herself out of the car. Bent double, she ran after Miss Morgan.

At first all she could see were bushes. Then, casting her eyes ahead, she glimpsed the woman walking briskly toward a group of oil storage tanks and a small building silhouetted against the starry sky. Several poles marched across the field with wires dangling aimlessly.

From trips she had taken into the country-side with her own and Kathy's father, Meg was sure this was an abandoned oilfield.

My friend the detective! Meg was full of anger and disappointment. What was Miss Morgan — Toad — up to now? Was Kathy in that dark building?

A bush crackled as Meg blundered into it. At once she crouched, fearful that the woman had heard the sound. Sure enough, when she peered cautiously through the branches, Miss Morgan was standing motionless, looking back.

As time went on and no footsteps came toward her, Meg glanced out again. This time the detective was hurrying toward the build-ing.

The bushes were becoming scarcer. Meg raced from cover to cover, her heart thudding from excitement and the rapid pace.

Now she had reached the first tank. Meg leaned against its side, grateful for its coolness against her cheek.

Miss Morgan's sturdy legs, covered by dark, baggy slacks, took her directly to a small building, actually only a shack, where tools and pump parts probably had once been stored. Meg heard the sharp rap of the woman's knuckles on the door. An unseen hand pulled it open, admitting the detective and affording a glimpse of the dimly lighted interior.

Leaving the shelter of the tank, Meg advanced toward the shack, poised to run for cover or drop to the ground if anyone came out.

Thin rays of light streaked from cracks and knotholes. Soon she could hear voices coming through the shabby walls. One was Miss Morgan's and the other, a man's. Meg crept closer and listened.

"So you got the ransom?" asked the man.

"Yes."

"Then let's go."

"She saw me," said Ann Morgan.

"So? She saw me and Bill."

The *she* must be Kathy. And apparently the man was Miss Morgan's partner. Meg clasped her thin arms around her chest to still her shaking. The lonely field and the harsh voices made her realize how helpless she was. How could she save her friend from these two?

"Quit stalling," said the man. "Turn the girl loose and let's split before the cops find us."

"No one followed me," snapped Miss Morgan.

Meg's last hope faded. She had thought one of the sheriff's deputies might have trailed the woman.

Ann Morgan was still talking. "You take care of the girl. I'll get the car started."

"Not me. I'm not risking any murder rap. Besides, she's a game kid."

There was a silence, broken by Miss Morgan's angry voice. "Get out of the way, then."

The man warned, "You use that gun and people will hear it for miles."

Meg started toward the door of the shack. She *had* to stop the woman.

Just as she stepped forward, she felt something touch her left knee, startling her so she jumped and had to clamp a hand over her mouth to keep from crying out. A small, familiar whimpering sound told her who had come. A warm body rubbed against her and a tail, whipping like a metronome, hit her leg. It was Rusty.

Hope flooded through her, comforting her whole body. Since Rusty was here, Kathy's father must be coming. Perhaps he had seen Miss Morgan pick up the ransom and had followed her. It would be like Rusty to leap out of the car as soon as the door opened and follow her trail across the field.

Meg reached down and found the dog's head. Gently she held his muzzle, the way Mr. Young did when he wanted him to be quiet. To her relief, it worked.

From inside the shack came sounds of thumping, followed by a thud as if someone had been thrown to the floor. A girl screamed, then suddenly was silent.

Meg had to do something. She gave the door a strong push, flinging it wide open.

Kathy was flat on her back on the floor. Ann Morgan was on top of her with both hands around her throat. Though Kathy was kicking and trying to push the woman away, Miss Morgan had the advantage in weight and muscle. A man Meg had never seen before stood in the shadows watching the struggle.

"Sic 'em!" cried Meg.

Before the words were out of her mouth, the dog shot into the room and leaped onto the woman, knocking her off Kathy onto the floor.

Meg started forward, but she had barely moved before the man — Miss Morgan's partner — crashed into her, throwing her to the ground as he bolted from the shack. Meg, dazed from the blow, sat up slowly.

Mr. Young's voice came from the darkness somewhere behind her, exclaiming, "Where d'you think you're going?" There was the sound of crashing in the bushes, and someone falling. He must have stopped the fleeing man.

Hearing his master's voice, Rusty turned his head. Instantly Miss Morgan sent the dog sprawling with a kick and leaped to her feet. She lunged for Kathy and pulled the girl in front of her like a shield.

Suddenly brilliant light flooded the shack. Over the noise of running footsteps, Meg heard Weaver's command: "Let go of her! We have you covered."

Miss Morgan shouted back, "I have *her* covered!" She had pulled a gun from her pocket and now held it against Kathy's head.

Meg moaned, "No . . . no!"

Showdown

Rusty, on his feet after Miss Morgan's kick, ran back toward her, growling, but she again let fly at him with her foot.

"Get that dog or this gun's going off!" she shouted.

Kathy's father appeared in the glare of light, and Meg saw Sheriff Weaver rush after him and pull him back. "Hold it, Dan," Weaver warned. "Have to take it easy. Just call the dog."

Mr. Young stopped uncertainly. Then, "Come here, Rusty," he ordered.

The dog took one more look at Kathy and the woman, then went to his master. Mr.

Young seized his collar and led him back into the shadows. Meg could just see them both, tense, watching Kathy and the woman.

Several deputies and Rangers were waiting nearby, ready to attack. But at the moment they were helpless.

Slowly Meg inched away from the door and got up. Her ankle hurt, and she limped over to where the sheriff and a Texas Ranger stood talking. She stopped near them, shivering, and listened in silence.

The Ranger was saying, "I have a man going behind the shack. If he can find a good knothole to poke his gun through, he'll try to distract her so we can rush her from the front."

"I'm afraid for Kathy," said Weaver. "If we could get her away from Morgan, I have a man — Robinson — who's a crack shot."

Just then the Ranger saw Meg. "For heaven's sake, girl. Get away from here!"

Weaver whirled around. "Meg! Go to my car!"

Meg started off slowly, thinking hard. After a few feet, she turned back and shook the sheriff's arm to get his attention. "I have an idea," she told him eagerly.

Weaver sounded irritated. "Don't bother me!"

"But, Sheriff! I can talk to Kathy with sign language!"

He frowned. "What d'you mean?"

"I can tell her what to do."

Weaver sighed. "All right. Let's hear it." He led her farther from the open doorway and the Ranger followed.

"Captain Jones, this is Meg Carberry, Kathy's best friend," explained the sheriff. "She must have hitched a ride with Morgan. What's your idea, Meg?"

"You want Kathy to get out of the way. I can tell her that in sign language."

The two men looked at each other. "It's risky," objected Weaver.

"Let me try it," begged Meg. "Miss Morgan isn't going to know what I'm saying to Kathy. She may not even notice."

Weaver stared at her. Then he patted her on the back. "Good girl. It might work. Let's try it."

"Right." Jones was quick and decisive. "The longer that woman holds the gun, the worse the chances are." He lowered his voice, "Meg, can you tell your friend to drop to the floor?"

"Sure. I can say that in sign language." She added nervously, "Maybe she can't do it, though. It depends on how hard Miss Morgan's hanging onto her."

"That's true." In spite of a cooling breeze that had come up, Weaver's forehead was beaded with perspiration. "But it's worth a try. We'll get Morgan's attention so she won't notice what you're doing. What can I say to her?"

Meg suggested, "You could tell her someone got the ransom money out of the car. They could do it. It's on the floor in front."

Jones gave Meg a look of approval. "That should get her attention. You've got a good head on you, girl!"

"Great!" The sheriff rubbed his hands together enthusiastically. "We found the money when we checked the car, so we're only telling her the truth."

Weaver immediately summoned Dan Young and Robinson, the crack shot, to brief them. Then Meg and the four men went over the details of the plan.

At first Mr. Young objected, afraid for Meg's safety, but finally he agreed.

As they talked, Meg could hear Miss Morgan shouting, "Get out of my way! Hurry up or I'll blast her."

As soon as they were sure they were ready to act, Meg and the three men approached the building where Miss Morgan, more furious than ever, still held Kathy at gunpoint.

Robinson, following the plan, went ahead to tell the Ranger who was holding the light to shift it just enough so Kathy would be able to see Meg clearly. He then walked back to the left into the shadow where he was out of Miss Morgan's sight, yet had a clear line of fire to her.

Weaver and the Ranger stayed slightly to the right, out of Robinson's way, standing so that their bodies shielded Meg but with enough space so she could look between them and see Kathy. Mr. Young and Rusty were farther to the right.

When the sheriff began to talk to the woman, Meg waved at her friend. Kathy looked steadily at her and her lips formed the word *Meg*.

"You're a hard driver to follow," Weaver said conversationally. "We'd have lost you way back if one of my men hadn't installed a beeper in your car."

The woman gave him a deadly glance. We were wrong when we named her Toad, thought Meg. She's a snake, a cobra.

The men in front of Meg moved slightly apart, and Weaver asked, "Say, Morgan, did you count the ransom money?"

This was Meg's signal. She lifted her left hand, palm up, in front of her chest. She knew

Kathy would understand that this was an indication she was going to talk in sign language.

Kathy didn't move, but her eyes were on Meg's hands.

Weaver said, "How did you happen to leave the ransom in the car? Tough luck for you. We have it now."

"What!" Toad exploded. For a moment it appeared she might turn the gun on Weaver. "Drop dead!" she spat at him.

This is it, thought Meg. All of the woman's attention was on the sheriff.

With the index and middle finger of her right hand Meg made a standing V in the palm of her left hand. Then she quickly let the V fall, palm up in the left hand. That meant *fall*. Next she pointed down with her index finger. In sign language, that was *down*.

With a quick motion, Kathy twisted out of Miss Morgan's arm and fell to the floor.

A shot rang out. Toad's gun flew across the room and she bent double, clutching her hand.

Meg ran to Kathy and helped her to her feet. They stood in the middle of the room, hugging each other and crying while the sheriff's men led Ann Morgan out of the shack.

There Goes Heron

That night Kathy, too tired to talk, went straight to bed, while Mr. Young put through a call to Meg's parents who were still vacationing in Switzerland. They hadn't even heard of the kidnapping.

"Kathy's home," Meg told them. "Yes, I'm fine, too. You don't have to come back. Stay and have fun."

The next morning breakfast at Bayview was late. Mrs. La Rose was there, answering the phone and doorbell and telling reporters that Kathy would talk to them at two that afternoon.

Over coffee, juice, scrambled eggs, and

doughnuts, Meg, Kathy, and Mr. Young pieced together all that had happened during the past few days.

Kathy sat at the head of the table where she could see the others' faces. Rusty lay on the floor beside her, as if afraid she would disappear again if he didn't keep watch.

They were still at the table at quarter to twelve when Sheriff Weaver arrived.

Meg poured him a cup of coffee and Mr. Young urged, "Have a doughnut, fresh this morning."

"Don't mind if I do." The sheriff took a chair next to him. "Did you hear the radio news?"

"No," answered Mr. Young. "We've been too busy talking."

"Then you don't know that Gabe turned himself in." The sheriff stirred cream and sugar into his coffee. "He came into the station about three this morning, shortly after I got back. Night before last, Morgan gave him orders to put Kathy out with chloroform and he didn't want to do it, so he took off, chloroform and all."

"He was good to me," said Kathy. "Go easy on him, please."

"I'll do what I can," Weaver promised. "He's been a help to us, too. He put the finger on the rest of the gang. Of course we had Harry, but we were able to pick up the other two this morning."

"There was a man on the shrimp boat — he was named Bill. He was good to me," Kathy told him. "I didn't like Harry, but at least he didn't kill me when Miss Morgan told him to."

"All right. We'll remember all that." Weaver helped himself to a second doughnut. "Besides, you'll have a chance to testify in court."

All during the conversation Meg had noticed how Kathy's eyes had gone from one speaker to the other. She seemed to understand almost everything that was said, not asking for help as often as usual.

Mrs. La Rose appeared in the doorway. "Is it all right if Julian comes in?"

"Sure," said Mr. Young. "Send him along."

Julian came in like a breeze from the bay. He hugged Kathy and Meg. "I'm sure glad to see you two all in one piece. I mean two pieces," he corrected himself. He stood back and looked at Kathy. "Who's your new hairdresser? Wow, some style job."

Kathy grinned and put her hand to her cropped hair. "It was free, too." She patted Rusty, who was wagging his tail at Julian. "I have one friend who doesn't care how I look."

Julian dropped onto the chair next to Meg.

Weaver smiled across at him. "You did a great job with the kidnap story."

"Thanks for having your secretary phone me to get down to the station." He glanced happily around the table. "My boss had the announcer mention my name on the air. I may get a bonus!"

Mr. Young said heartily, "Good. Hope you do. And Sheriff, after the way you handled this case, you'll have no trouble at election time. I know *I'll* work for you."

Weaver looked pleased. "Thanks, Dan. I may make Meg my deputy."

Meg reddened. "I know. I had everything wrong. I was sure Tripp was the kidnapper, and I was a big help to Miss Morgan, of all people."

Weaver chuckled. "She had me fooled, too. The way she put the finger on Essie Prentice for leaking news sold me."

Julian cut in. "I learned something more about Essie. Her mother told my mother Essie always wanted to be a reporter but she hasn't had any luck getting a job."

"Aha!" said Dan Young. "So she fed information to the TV reporters and I suppose the newspapers, too, trying to prove what a good news gatherer she could be."

"What about Miss Morgan?" asked Meg. "You said she had you fooled."

Weaver nodded. "I watched her from the first on general principles. But I began to get suspicious when she tried to convince me Tripp was guilty. He's an odd character but we were keeping an eye on him and we *knew* he was innocent. Then Morgan really blew her cover when she snatched you out of the Ogden house, Kathy, and took you to that shack."

"How'd you know she did that?" asked Meg.

"We didn't know all the details until Gabe told us. But we did figure out she had been up to something when we found the blue panel truck yesterday afternoon abandoned on a side street in Brighton, after one of the Rangers saw her get off the Brighton bus in Oak Point, early in the morning."

Meg's fingers flew. Weaver was talking too fast and was forgetting to keep his face toward Kathy.

He went on, a trifle more slowly. "What we didn't know was that Gabe phoned her when Kathy broke the window, and she trotted straight over to the Ogden house on foot. Gave our man the slip. For a few hours we didn't know where she'd gone."

Kathy asked, "Then after she drove me to

the shack, she took the truck to Brighton and left it there?"

"That's right," said Weaver. "She didn't dare drive it back to Oak Point. She didn't want anyone to know she had any connection with Gabe or the other men. You see, she's the mastermind. Stays in the background and collects the money. She's smart. Smart enough to send us to search the Ogden house *before* they hid Kathy there."

"She *is* a detective, isn't she?" asked Meg.

"Yes. I checked that out. But when I began to have doubts about her, I phoned back to her home city. That time I got the police chief, himself, and he said, 'We don't have anything definite on her. But we're beginning to suspect she had a hand in a kidnap case six months ago. Watch her!' Apparently she led two lives."

"Why didn't you tell me?" demanded Meg. She felt rather peeved that she hadn't been given the true story.

"I didn't dare. It was important for you to keep on treating her like a trusted friend so she wouldn't guess we were onto her." Weaver picked up his cup and drank the last of his coffee.

Mr. Young puzzled, "I don't see why Morgan told Meg she was going to follow Tripp."

Weaver put down his cup. "I believe she was setting up an alibi in case we saw her at the ransom pickup site."

"Could be." Mr. Young looked thoughtful. "I guess you never dreamed Meg would hide out in the woman's car. That was a dangerous thing to do, Meg."

"I know. I'll never do anything like that again. But I wanted to be there when Kathy was set free."

"I'm glad you were," Kathy spoke up. Her hands went to her neck. "I might not be here if you and Rusty hadn't come in when you did."

Meg made a face at her and finger-spelled the word *Mush*.

"I agree with Kathy," said Weaver. "We might have been seconds too late to save her." He smiled affectionately at Kathy. "You don't look any the worse for all of this. I believe you have more self-confidence than before."

"I think I do," agreed Kathy. "Ever since I got deaf I've been afraid to go anyplace without Dad or Meg because I thought I couldn't understand people. But I figure I won't get into many situations as bad as what happened the last few days, so I think I can manage." She looked at her father. "I've decided I'd like to go to that art workshop in Brighton."

Her father beamed. "That *almost* makes all of this worthwhile." He met Meg's eyes. "Looks as if our bird is leaving the nest."

Kathy leaned toward Meg. "I still wish you were going with me."

Meg knew her friend was afraid she felt left out. She hastened to reassure her. "I'd be a total loss in an art workshop. You'll have a great time."

Julian put his arm around Meg's shoulders. "I'll look after this girl. It'll be a pleasure."

Mrs. La Rose appeared in the doorway. "Come here! Quick! Look on the road!"

With Rusty in the lead, they all rushed to the terrace in time to see two cars drive by with horns blowing. The second car was decorated with crepe paper ribbons. In the back seat Meg glimpsed a woman in a white dress and veil, and next to her a man so tall his head was almost against the ceiling of the car.

"Who's that?" asked Mr. Young.

Mrs. La Rose smiled. "Mr. Tripp and Essie Prentice got married this morning."

The sheriff groaned. "Poor guy. He isn't getting much of a prize."

Kathy came up beside Meg. "There goes Heron," she said.

Meg turned to her friend. "He'll never know what a big part he played in our kidnap case!"